Fay Weldon was born in England and raised in New Zealand. She took degrees in Economics and Psychology at the University of St Andrews in Scotland and after a decade of odd jobs and hard times began writing fiction. She is now well known as novelist, screenwriter and cultural journalist. Her novels include *The Life and Loves of a She-Devil*, *Puffball*, *The Cloning of Joanna May*, *Affliction*, *Worst Fears*, *Big Women* and *Rhode Island Blues*. She has several collections of short stories to her name: her latest being *A Hard Time To Be a Father* and she has also written a collection of essays, *Godless in Eden*. Fay Weldon lives in London.

Also by Fay Weldon

Fiction

THE FAT WOMAN'S JOKE
DOWN AMONG THE WOMEN
FEMALE FRIENDS
REMEMBER ME
LITTLE SISTERS
PRAXIS
PUFFBALL
THE PRESIDENT'S CHILD
THE LIFE AND LOVES
  OF A SHE-DEVIL
THE SHRAPNEL ACADEMY
THE HEART OF THE
  COUNTRY
THE HEARTS AND LIVES
  OF MEN
THE RULES OF LIFE
LEADER OF THE BAND
THE CLONING OF JOANNA
  MAY
DARCY'S UTOPIA
GROWING RICH
LIFE FORCE
AFFLICTION
SPLITTING
WORST FEARS
BIG WOMEN
RHODE ISLAND BLUES

Children's Books

WOLF THE
  MECHANICAL DOG
NOBODY LIKES ME

Short Story Collections

WATCHING ME,
  WATCHING YOU
POLARIS
MOON OVER MINNEAPOLIS
WICKED WOMEN
A HARD TIME
  TO BE A FATHER

Non-fiction

LETTERS TO ALICE
REBECCA WEST
SACRED COWS
GODLESS IN EDEN

FAY WELDON

The Bulgari Connection

Flamingo
An Imprint of HarperCollins*Publishers*
77–85 Fulham Palace Road,
Hammersmith, London W6 8JB

Flamingo ® is a registered trade mark of
HarperCollins*Publishers* Ltd

www.fireandwater.com

Published by Flamingo 2001
1 3 5 7 9 8 6 4 2

First published by BVLGARI Italy S.p.A. 2000
as a special limited gift edition

This novel is entirely a work of fiction.
The names, characters and incidents portrayed in it are
the work of the author's imagination. Any resemblance to
actual persons, living or dead, events or localities is
entirely coincidental.

A catalogue record for this book
is available from the British Library

ISBN 0 00 712126 1

Typeset in Sabon by Palimpsest Book Production Limited,
Polmont, Stirlingshire

Printed and bound in Great Britain by
Omnia Books Limited, Glasgow

1

Doris Dubois is twenty-three years younger than I am. She is slimmer than I am, and more clever. She has a degree in economics, and hosts a TV arts programme. She lives in a big house with a swimming pool at the end of a country lane. It used to be mine. She has servants and a metal security gate which glides open when her little Mercedes draws near. I tried to kill her once, but failed.

When Doris Dubois comes into a room all heads turn: she has a sunny disposition and perfect teeth. She smiles a lot and most people find themselves returning the smile. If I did not hate her I expect I would quite like her. She is, after all, the nation's sweetheart. My husband loves her, and can see no fault in her. He buys her jewels.

The swimming pool is covered, warmed, and flanked by marble tiles and can be used summer and winter. Trees and shrubs in containers have been placed all around the pool area. In photographs – and the press come often to see how Doris Dubois lives – the pool seems to exist in a mountain grotto.

The water has to be cleaned of leaves more often than any pool of mine ever did. But who's counting cost?

Doris Dubois swims in her pool every morning, and twice a week my ex-husband Barley dives in to swim beside her. I have had them watched by detectives. After their swim servants come and offer warmed white towels into which they snuggle with little cries of joy. I have heard these cries on tape, as well as other more important, more profound, less social cries, those noises men and women make when they abandon rationality and throw in their lot with nature. '*Cris de jouissance*', the French call them. *Défense d'émettre des cris de jouissance*, I read once on a bedroom wall in a French hotel when Barley and I were in our heyday, and went on our humble holidays so happily together. In the days when we thought love would last forever, when we were poor, when joy was on the agenda.

Défense d'émettre des cris de jouissance. They had a hope!

Barley has aged better than I have. I smoked and drank and lay in the sun during the years of our happiness, on this Riviera and that, and my skin has dried out dreadfully and the doctor will not let me take what he calls artificial hormones. I get them through the Internet but do not tell either my doctor or my psychoanalyst this. The former would warn me against them and the latter would tell me to find my inner self before attending to the outer. Sometimes I worry about the dosage I take, but not often. I have other things to worry about.

2

'It's too bad,' said Doris to Barley as they lay beside one another in a tumbled pile of white cotton and lace bedclothes, in a vast bed whose elegant top and tail had been designed, even though not made, by the great Giacometti himself, 'that that murderess should still be using your name.'

'Murderess might be too strong,' said Barley amiably, 'Murderous, was how the Judge described her.'

'The difference is only marginal,' said Doris. 'The fact that I am still alive is due to me and not to her. My foot still hurts. I think you should get your lawyers on to it. It's absurd that after divorce women should be allowed to keep their husband's name. They should revert to the one they had before they married: they should cut their losses and start over. Otherwise the mistakes of one's youth – like marriage to the wrong person – can hang around to haunt you forever. I speak for her sake, as well as my own, and indeed yours. While she calls herself Salt she is bound to attract headlines.'

'It seems a little hard to take away Gracie's name,' said Barley. 'I was the only claim to fame she ever had. She was a schoolgirl when I met her: a schoolgirl she remained, at heart. A man such as myself needs a little sophistication in his partner.'

'I hate it when you call her Gracie,' said Doris. 'I want you only ever to refer to her as your ex-wife.'

Grace Salt had started life as Dorothy Grace McNab, but Barley had preferred Grace to Dorothy, Dorothy reminding him of Judy Garland in *The Wizard of Oz*, so Grace she had become.

Doris had not started life as Doris Dubois but as Doris Zoac, right down there at the end of the alphabet where no-one looks except the taxman, and had changed it by deed poll the better to further her media ambitions. She had never got round to telling Barley this, and the longer she put it off the harder it got to say.

'It seems a little hard to take my ex-wife's name away,' said Barley, obediently. He, who exercised power over so many, took particular pleasure in being bossed around by Doris. They both giggled a little, from the sheer naughtiness of it all, of being happy.

Doris Dubois wore her jewellery to bed, for Barley. He loved that. He loved not just the sight of it, white gold and pavé diamonds, cold metal intricately, beautifully worked, lain heavily against the cool, moist flesh of wrist and throat, but he loved the feel of it. Last night as his hand had strayed over her breasts, their nipples peaked in reassuring response, and up to feel the tenderness of her mouth, his fingers had encountered the smooth, hard edge of metal, and his whole body had been startled into instant response. Sometimes Barley was mildly worried by the people who said to him, vulgarly, 'Oh well, what does age matter, there's always Viagra when the newness wears off,' but eighteen months on there was no sign of it doing so. Doris kept Barley young: and the gifts he gave her were by the very nature of their giving returned – not by way of bribe or payment, but as tokens of simple adoration. Barley was fifty-eight years old, and Doris was thirty-two.

3

I must face the truth about Doris Dubois. She reflects fame and status on my husband, as he does on her, and he cannot resist it. What chance have I? She is the darling of the media: now they are an item Barley has his picture in *Hello!* and *Harper's & Queen*, and a fine handsome couple they make. She with her bosom hanging out of Versace and her throat so white and elegant, ringed with bright jewels: he with his thick grey hair, broad shoulders and strong industrial jaw. When Barley was with me he never rose above *The Developers' and Builders' Bulletin*, although once he did make the cover. But he is ambitious: it was not enough for him: he can't stay still. It was *Hello!* or bust.

Barley is one of those well-built men with graven features who rise to positions of great power: his jaw has grown squarer through the years. Even his hair has stayed thick as it greys. He is a master of men, and it shows. If the world is ever to see the cloning of humans, these are the pair that should be chosen to make it a better place. I said as much to my psychotherapist, Dr Jamie Doom, the other day and he congratulated me on my insight.

*   *   *

Twelve months after our parting, six months after our divorce, I have stopped trying to convince myself and others that in losing Barley I have lost nothing of value. I no longer describe him to others, after the vulgar manner of so many deserted spouses, as selfish, bullying, mean, unreasonable, hopelessly neurotic, even insane. He is none of these things. Barley, like Doris, is kind, good and perceptive, clever and handsome, and capable of great love. It's just that he gives it to her, not me.

4

'The fact is that your ex-wife does not deserve your name,' said Doris after breakfast. Once she got an idea into her head it tended to stay there. 'She is violent and aggressive and full of hate and spite.'

They ate on the terrace, in the early sun. Doris had to be at the studio by ten, and Barley at a meeting of the Confederation of British Industry likewise. Doris's Philippine maid Maria served decaff and fruit, calories carefully weighed and counted by Doris's nutritionist. Barley's chauffeur Ross would have a flask of real coffee and a bacon sandwich ready in the back of the car when he turned up to collect Barley.

'I hear you,' said Barley, whose lawyer had told him it would look better in the divorce courts if he could claim to have seen a counsellor. The law these days favoured those who put in an appearance of wanting to save their marriages, and the suggestion of a basic incompatibility with Grace would be more helpful to his case than the simple wanting to go off with Doris Dubois, a younger woman. As ever, Barley had

turned time otherwise wasted to good account, and was now
adept at the language of understanding and compassion. 'Best
to let it out. And I feel for your distress. But you did emerge
from the incident more or less undamaged.'

And indeed, Doris Dubois was the least damaged creature he
had ever seen, let alone taken to bed: long lean tanned limbs;
centred by the kind of full, well nippled bosom most skinny
women achieve only after implants, but for Doris a blessing of
birth – her breasts still retaining the warm consoling texture
of human flesh. Her mouth curved sweetly: she had wide
blue eyes into which Barley could stare without embarrassment. Doris had developed the media art of paying attention
to something else altogether while looking and smiling and
nodding; he could hold her eye without actually holding it,
as it were, and he found that liberating. Intense love can so
often have its own embarrassments. She was widely informed:
he liked that. He had spent too much of his life with Gracie,
who never read a novel and whose idea of a conversation was
'yes, dear', and 'what did you say, dear?' and 'where were
you last night?', who lay passively and compliantly on her
back during sex. He had forgotten what the life of the mind
was like. Most women, he had noticed, whose looks assure
them of acceptance and approval from infancy, neglected their
intelligence and sensitivities, as did Grace – but not so Doris:
Doris could hold her own at any dinner party in the land. She
was perhaps a little humourless, but like a Persian rug of great
quality, there must be some flaw in the design, or else God will
be offended.

'All that aside,' observed Doris Dubois, '– and not that I
want to marry you, marriage being such an old-fashioned
institution, and I would always rather be known as Doris

9

Dubois, rather than Doris Salt, I couldn't bear to be so near the end of the alphabet – nevertheless, if I were to be your legal married wife, and not just your partner, I would not want there to be another Mrs Salt around.'

Barley Salt felt his heart contract with joy. He had done the best he could with the cards dealt to him at birth – but there were still dinner tables at which he felt inadequate, at which he felt people laughed at him, for the rude, crude fellow he had been born. If the conversation turned to opera, or literature, or art, he felt at a loss. To be actually married to Doris Dubois, so at ease in all these areas of life, would be triumph indeed. And she, for all her disclaimers, had brought the matter up, not he.

5

What is this? A letter through the post from Barley's solicitors? He wants to deny me my name? He wants to rob me of my very self? I must no longer be Grace Salt? Extra alimony offered – £500 a week – if I revert to my maiden name? (At least he bribes, he doesn't threaten.) I must hurl myself back to my unmarried state and be seventeen again and that long lost creature Grace McNab? I can't remember who she was. How can this be, what have I done, am I so worthless that he can't endure me to have so much as a past that's linked with his? I must wink out of existence altogether? Well, I can understand it. Look at me! Described as murderous by the Judge, labelled a would-be murderer: Barley must feel he is entitled to protect himself and her. Of course he wishes to obliterate me. What am I but an hysterical woman who once performed a senseless and gratuitous act of violence – I quote the Judge – and deserve no better. A man may seek the authenticity of his feelings, as our one-time marriage counsellor described my husband's love for Doris Dubois, but a woman must not.

'*Judge Rubs Salt into Grace's Wounds,*' said the headlines.

'*Lovesick Drama of Fat-Cat Spouse*,' and so on. '*TV Culture Queen Stole My Man, alleges Salt Wife*'. A hundred faces crowding in on me with phallic lenses and popping bulbs as they hurried me, distraught and disgraced, blanket over my head, to the police cells. By the time I emerged, greyer and fatter by a year and a quarter, the media had lost interest; only a couple of film crews, some local journalists, and a woman's group wanting a donation were waiting. The authorities kindly let me out the back entrance, so that even my lawyer missed me, and I had to make my own way home. Or what I now was to call home: Tavington Court, a great block of apartments in Victorian red brick behind the British Museum, where sad divorcées hide, and little old ladies grateful for the protection of the resident porter, and widows living their leftover lives in genteel loneliness. It takes up a whole street and those who have grandchildren to visit are lucky. I am not so lucky. My son Carmichael is not likely to oblige.

All my conversations at the time were with lawyers and accountants and all they seemed to want me to think about was the prospect of age and infirmity and death in the future.
I was victorious, but only to live my leftover life alone. And I didn't suppose Carmichael wanted me out in Sydney – 'to be near my son' – embarrassing him.

The media have lost interest in me altogether now. They are happy for Barley and Doris's happiness. They were married last week. The wedding was in *Hello!*, and I hear put the circulation up no end. My plight becomes yesterday's fish and chip wrappings. As Doris would be the first to point out, how that dates me! Fish and chips are not eaten from newsprint now, the EC would never allow it, but if sold at all, out of recyclable polyethylene cartons. I don't like eating alone in restaurants, sitting there with my book, feeling the pity of others. It is quite astonishing how few people I know. My married life revolved around Barley: the people we knew, knew us as a couple. I was just the tag-along. They feel sorry for me now and when the kind people, as I think of them, do ask me round, it is to lunch not dinner and we normally eat in the kitchen. It is better than nothing.

I have lost the art of conversation. Once I was quite good at it, but after years of living with Barley who always waxed so noisy and indignant if ever I said anything more than yes dear, no dear, I learned the prudence of silence, and in the end he took me for a fool. And there certainly wasn't much snappy dialogue in prison and for awhile after I came out I was struck quite dumb, and had to search for words with which to express my thoughts at all.

Doris Dubois is anything but dumb. I do not watch her show: it is too painful for me: but sometimes flicking through the channels I forget and come across her, fronting her highly successful *Artsworld Extra*. It's on twice a week. Nine o'clock peak time Thursdays. Late night repeat, Mondays. Her perfect figure, the bouncy, short cropped hair, her startling smile, the ease with which she handles ideas, the evident intelligence, the breadth of information, the flying sound bites – the worst you can say about her is that she looks like a Captain of Hockey on speed. And why, unless you have special reason, should you say the worst of her? Even I have trouble doing so.

Doris Dubois now has Barley's name – though I notice she doesn't even bother to use it – as well as his love, his time, his attention and his money. I have the couple followed from time to time by a detective, one Harry Bountiful. What a splendid name! I chose him because of it, flicking through the Yellow Pages. Doris and Barley will meet up in Aspreys in Bond Street, then drift over to Gucci's where Barley will perhaps buy a pair of loafers, the better to walk through St James's Park and feed the ducks. Then perhaps they will call in at Apsley House, address No.1, London, built for the Duke of Wellington, the one who defeated Napoleon. There they will see the fine equestrian painting of the Duke by Goya. If they look hard they will see the faint shadow of a tricolor hat beginning to show through the surface paint. The portrait was originally of 'King' Joseph Bonaparte of Spain, Napoleon's brother. But the Duke and his victorious troops were at the gates of Madrid, the usurper had fled, so Goya prudently painted a new head on the body, and sold it to the Duke. An artist has to live. Why waste a perfectly good horse?

Or perhaps Barley and Doris, hand in hand, will drift off to Bulgari in Sloane Street, to stare at some ruby imbedded steel circlet for her slim arm, wondering whether they will or whether they won't, but mostly that they will. Because she deserves it. Because she is *her*. They will stroll along to South Ken., and the Victoria and Albert Museum to study, say, the Sèvres dinner service (1848) that was once Queen Victoria's own, and Doris will explain its fineness to him, and the curator will even let them handle the settings. They are an important couple, and she has friends in high cultural places.

It is thanks to his new wife that Barley can now judge the quality even of the plates set before him, tell china from pottery, and understand how the two can never merge. He knows now where camp begins and crassness stops. Doris is Barley's living Fine Arts programme. They are in love; perhaps they give more time and attention to each other than either can spare. Her ratings drop just a little: his dividends falter. Because meanwhile, as Harry Bountiful puts it, the real world goes on. But this couple, newly discovered to one another, is blessed. Strokes of good fortune come their way. Last week Doris got five numbers in the lottery and won twelve hundred pounds. Barley's latest office block won an architectural prize. Perhaps Doris was close to one of the judges.

I tried to explain to the Court that it was not that I hated Doris, just that I wanted Barley to realise the intensity of my distress and desperation.

'You really thought,' enquired Judge Tobias Longue, 'that if you ran down your husband's mistress in a car park he would be sorry for you? Then you have lived a long time yet don't know men very well. Good Lord, woman, he will have every excuse now for leaving you. You played into his hands.' Tobias Longue was one of those lawyers who write thrillers, and had only recently been promoted to the bench. He had an eye and an ear for drama. He was both on my side, and not. There had been no witnesses. It was Doris's word against mine. At the very worst, I told the Court, Doris had wrenched her ankle as she leapt out of the way of my Jaguar: but see how now she limped into court, pale and grave and prattling forgiveness.

'She's not in her right mind,' Doris told Judge Tobias Longue. 'I caught a glimpse of her face through the windscreen, her teeth bared, her mad eyes staring, just as the wheel went over my foot, and I felt this terrible pain and passed out. My fear as I fell was that she'd reverse back over me and crush me to death beneath that heavy car. She needs treatment, not punishment. She is unbalanced to the point of paranoia, an obsessive-compulsive. She suffers from pathological jealousy. I first met her husband when he appeared on my cultural review show: we are involved as colleagues in the setting up of a Cable TV company. But that's all there is to it: good heavens, Barley Salt is a quarter of a century older than I am, and I regard him as a father.'

She spoke eloquently and persuasively, as was her trade. I stumbled through my few words. Of course she was believed.

Later she said to the Press, 'Poor Mrs Salt. I'm afraid she belongs to the past, one of those prurient women who assume that if a man and a woman are alone in a room together, something sexual's bound to happen.' The Press forgot conveniently, when writing up the wedding, that at the time of the trial Barley and Doris vehemently denied any romantic involvement. Of course there was, starting from the very beginning in the Green Room, after everyone else had gone home, after she'd had him on her show, talking about the necessity of sponsorship of the arts by big business. I had watched that interview as a proud wife should, and seen the way she looked at him, the way his body inclined towards hers. He didn't come home until early morning, and when he got into bed he smelt of TV studios, static electricity, sex and something else sickly and evil I couldn't identify.

The prosecution asked for five years, I got three and served only fifteen months. In the event the Judge was less vindictive than anyone else around. At least he acknowledged the provocation. He said in his summing up it was a silly attempt with a car outside a supermarket and that Doris had jumped easily enough out of the way. And it's true, she has perfect knees, being only thirty-three years old. At fifty-five, I already have one that is arthritic, though I didn't let it stand in my way when I put the accelerator down. The pain in the heart is always worse than the one in the body.

It has taken me a year with Dr Jamie Doom the TV psychotherapist – he does take a few patients privately – to be able to face the facts of the matter. Doris Dubois is a superior human being to myself in every way and no sane man would not prefer her to me, in bed or out of it, as wife, partner or mistress. I face myself in the mirror, I look at my fading eyes and know that they have seen too much, and that there is no brightening them. What ages us is experience: there can be no forgetfulness.

'But aren't you angry?' asks Dr Jamie Doom, 'You must try to find your anger.' But I can't.

Perhaps God will reward me for having come to terms, as Dr Doom puts it, with my distress. I am sure no-one else will. This evening I am going to a party given by a pair of the kind ones, Lady Juliet Random and her husband Sir Ronald. It's a charity auction in aid of 'Lost Children Somewhere'. I am invited not just out of kindness but because I might be able to give a hundred pounds or so to Lady Juliet's cause. Nothing compared to the thousands others give – I am only fifth or sixth division wealth now that I live on alimony – but no doubt still worth the champagne and canapés which I'll consume. At least I don't have to worry about meeting Doris and Barley at Sir Ronald's: they move in more elevated artistic and political circles now. The parties they go to are attended by Arts Ministers, Leisure Gurus, Museum Moguls, Dotcom-Millionaires, Monarchs of the BBC and so forth. I tell you what, every now and then I could take Barley by surprise and make him laugh. I think Doris can do everything for Barley but that. She is too intent on pleasuring herself and him to have time for much mirth. But I daresay with age even my laughter, which once Barley loved, will turn into a witch's cackle.

6

'Who is the woman sitting in the corner?' young Walter Wells asked Lady Juliet.

He had been studying her. She sat at rest as though posing for a portrait. He thought she looked lovely, whoever she was. She was not as young as she had been, it was true, but this gave her looks a kind of lush and wistful melancholy: he had been much taken in his childhood by images of the blown rose, of battered scarlet velvet petals, tempest tossed. Walter Wells thought perhaps he had been born a poet almost as much as an artist. Though now, at twenty-nine, he earned a living painting portraits, he sometimes felt that his heart was in language rather than in the image. But a man, however multi-talented, can't do everything and the image paid better than words in the new century. So many languages it was only polite to learn, from Urdu to Serbo-Croat, that everyone had settled for symbols. A flat hand to stop you crossing the road was better than the word STOP, a green running man to show you the way out preferable to the word EXIT. So he had been practical and gone to art college, only to find the artist was as likely to live in a garret as the poet, unless he was very lucky.

It was in pursuit of luck that he was here at this charity auction today, where he knew no-one and felt altogether out of his generation. He it was who had painted the portrait of Lady Juliet Random, which was any minute now to be auctioned for the sake of Little Children, Everywhere, Lady Juliet's favourite charity. He liked Lady Juliet and wanted to oblige her, she was good looking and relaxed and easy to paint and had only good things to say about everyone. She was quite voluptuous, and Walter Wells wished more of his sitters were like her. A good curve painted well, but in his experience if you blessed your sitters with a roundness of line on the canvas they only accused you of making them look fat.

'Who can you mean?' asked Lady Juliet. 'The woman in the crushed velvet dress? Good Lord, that kind of fabric went out thirty years ago. But I'm glad to see she's making an effort. It's poor Grace Salt, the one who tried to mow down Doris Dubois in her Jaguar in a supermarket car park. You must have heard of her? No?'

'No.'

'Oh, you artists! Snug in your garrets, safe from the world.' Walter's portrait of Lady Juliet was to be the centrepiece of the auction. He had actually painted two, one which Lady Juliet would keep, the other a copy for the auction, painted for free, his gift in kind to Little Children, Everywhere. Lady Juliet had twisted his arm and melted his heart, as she was so good at doing, her soft mouth imploring, her eyes beseeching: he had done the extra work and not complained, though she had not even offered to pay for paint or canvas. People did not realise that these things cost money. The Randoms were pleased with the painting: they would hang it in pride of place on the wall of their library in their Eaton Square house, one of those stoic well-built cream-painted places with stolid pillars and steps and an air of infinite dullness, but at least he would know where it was. The copy would go to an unknown home. He did not like that.

'The Salt scandal was in all the papers,' said Lady Juliet, taking his arm, as she did at every opportunity. She was looking magnificent and charming both: such an art to be so grand and yet loveable, and thus to inspire in others more admiration than envy. She had a smooth, untroubled childish face, with small even features and a curved mouth given to laughter, and if she had nothing nice to say she kept silent, which was more than most in her circle did. She was dressed tonight as she had been for the portrait, in simple slinky white and her plentiful probably blonde hair twisted on top of her head. Clasped round her neck, falling in roundels of bright colour against her firm, creamy skin was a Bulgari necklace, steel and gold set with cabochon emeralds, rubies, sapphires and brilliant cut diamonds, made in the sixties, and insured for £275,000, a sum Walter had heard mentioned as he worked.

Sir Ronald had charged more than once into the garden room, clouding the good North light with cigar smoke as was his habit, and doubted the wisdom of the jewels not being in the bank, couldn't Walter work from a photograph? But Lady Juliet had said authenticity was so important, lights should not be hidden in bushels, jewels could not be forever in vaults or they lost their magic, what was the point of having these things if the world didn't know about it, and so on. What was he afraid of? That Walter would run off with them? Slip the matching earrings into his pocket? Walter was too poetic a soul to run off with anything. He was an artist, everyone knew artists were above material things.

Which they obviously believed in their naivety, since Walter was being paid only £1800 to do the portrait – well, actually to do the two – and the Randoms assumed that was generous, and that they were doing him a kindness, employing and trusting a comparative unknown in the first place, introducing him to those levels of society where artists got more like £18,000 for a single fashionable portrait, than £1800 for a pair, which worked out at £300 a week for six weeks work. He would rather paint landscapes when it came to it: the weather kept changing and the light with it, but at least the landscape sat still.

'So you want to be introduced to the woman in the corner in the crushed velvet dress,' said Lady Juliet, ever happy to oblige. The jewels in her necklace glittered and glanced where they caught the light: the thing seemed magically, beautifully alive; he hoped he had got the intensity of it on the canvas: paint and brush could do only so much. But on the whole he was pleased. The copy, he thought, had been minimally better than the original: he had really got his hand in on the precious stones second time round, but he was the only one who would notice that. Only one in a hundred ever really noticed anything.

'You only have ten minutes before the auction begins,' said Lady Juliet. 'I'm going to want you to go on stage and talk to them a little about art, and be altogether as languid and beautiful as you can, not that you have to try. They'll think you're photogenic and have a future and prices will triple. But do by all means talk to Grace first. I need her in a good mood. Barley gave her a good settlement, at least three million, and probably more, none of us like talking large figures in the press or they take us for fat cats, and I do so hate being called fat, even though I know I am. Little Children, Everywhere need women like Grace. The wretched of the earth could do with some of everyone's alimony. This is the growth area, the future lies in this world of multiple divorces, multiple remarriages. Not just money to charity on death, but on divorce, too, an intrinsic part of any settlement. We all live far too well, with our champagne and our canapés, don't you think? But what's to be done? The world is what it is. All we can do is change our little corner of it.'

And so Walter Wells was introduced to Grace Salt at the Randoms' charity do. There was the same difference between their ages as there was between Doris and Barley. Twenty-six years separated Grace and Walter, twenty-six years separated Doris and Barley.

Walter saw a woman with sad, dark, glowing eyes and a gentle, surprised expression, as if she was seeing the world for the first time. It was the same look a baby has, when it's about twelve months old, and has learned that in order to walk and run you have to develop an indifference to sharp corners. He thought she was perhaps about forty: older than he was at any rate but who was counting? Her dress was in crushed deep crimson velvet, a texture and colour he longed to get on canvas. She wore it buttoned up to the neck and its long sleeves ended in sedate cuffs, as if she needed what small protection from the world even fabric could bring her. She wore no jewellery, other than small pearl stud earrings, on the kind of clips which bite the ear.

Of course he had thought of roses: his mother, a clergyman's wife, had grown a wonderfully scented rose of that colour in the rectory garden where he had spent so much of his childhood. His mother had told him that its name was Flower

23

of Jerusalem: a rather ordinary pink as a virginal bud, but deepening into crimson with every week of its flowering, until the petals were all but black, falling away, splaying, from the precious stameny centre they had once guarded so tightly.

Grace Salt sat alone, listening to the string quartet which played beneath a kind of pink plaster portico set above a blue transparent dais, lighted from beneath, which gave the players a ghostly glow. A firm called Fund Raisers Fun had provided it, along with little gold chairs, champagne and canapés, and it sat oddly indeed amongst the staid chintz, dull antiques and solid worth of the rest of the house.

He sat next to her on the green shot silk sofa. She forgot his name a second after Lady Juliet had introduced them, and gone, but politely asked him about himself. He said he was the painter of the portrait which was to be the centrepiece of the auction. She said she liked it very much: he had brought out Lady Juliet's kindness. 'Lady Juliet doesn't want to look just kind,' said Walter. 'She'd rather be seen as significant. I tried to make her look severe, but alas, it's the art of the portrait painter to bring out the soul of the sitter, and it is what it is.' He had developed this line only an hour ago for the benefit of the handful of gossip columnists who'd blessed the evening with their presence. Walter had thought it was perhaps rather clichéd but they'd gone for it.
'I know Lady Juliet is kind,' said Grace, 'because she asks me round to lunch quite often. Not kind enough to ask me to dinner, of course. But then unpartnered women, if they have no particular talent, or style, are so much a waste of an expensive place setting they quite offend the sumptuary laws.'

Walter's father the rector had often spoken of the sumptuary laws when Walter had wanted a bicycle or new trainers, which other village children could not afford. Conspicuous consumption had always been seen as an offence to God and Man: in the Middle Ages actual laws were enforced. Spend too much too loosely and you got punished. Walter had not heard mention of the sumptuary laws since his father's death, and though they had irritated him most profoundly at the time, they had now entered into the nostalgic narrative which composed the memory of his father. He felt she would understand his heart.

He said he was sure she could find a partner if she wanted one. A woman as beautiful as she. 'You are so gallant,' she said, 'and quite absurd. You remind me of my son Carmichael.' But she cheered up a little, and smiled at him with a kind of hazy half smile he found enchanting, and as if she now actually saw him. He liked her voice, it was croaky and deep, as if she had spent a lifetime drinking and smoking, though now she refused the waiter's offer of champagne and took mineral water instead.

He thought he would like to see her face on the pillow next to him when he woke up in the morning. Those he so often saw were brutal in their confidence and self-esteem, the smooth texture of their skin unmarked by weariness or doubt. They bored him. He felt as old as her, or older, betrayed by a body which demonstrated all the vigour of youth, ill-matched to a soul which already felt jaded and world weary. And she would not ask him questions as they did, the ones who moved into his cold attic studio, lured by his looks and his easels and the romance of squeezed oil paints on stained wooden tables, and the unmade brass bed; but who within weeks would be jealous of his attention to canvas and not to them, and implying that painting was not a proper job. Off they'd go, to their smart

25

well-appointed offices in publishing, or PR, or advertising or wherever, for a return on their labour far greater than any he was ever likely to achieve. And one evening they would simply not come home, but within a couple of days a brother, or some gay friend, or a father would turn up to take away their possessions.

That the studio had a good North light, that crackling cold for some reason increased intensity of colour, had apparently not impressed them: the tenderness of his lovemaking could not make up for his reluctance to turn up the central heating. It had happened enough times – well, twice in as many months, within the last year – to make him feel this was to be the pattern of life and there was nothing much to be done about it. Yet he hated living alone. Art made a frugal bed companion. An older woman would surely be more sensitive as to how he lived, why he lived. It was true the skin round her jaw sagged a little, and curved lines ran between her cheeks and the corners of her mouth, and the division between lip and the rest was a trifle blurred, but she was the proper shape for a woman. He wanted to paint her. He wanted to be in her presence. He wanted her in his bed. Good Lord, he thought, this is love at first sight. He felt the need for a cigarette. He asked, nervously, if she minded. She had once, she said, been practically a chain smoker; but she had given it up in prison. It was so terrible in there it hadn't seemed to matter if it was a few degrees more terrible still. He should go ahead. She didn't mind.
'Prison! What for . . .' Walter was startled.
'Attempted murder,' she said.

Lady Juliet swooped and carried Walter Wells off, like a cat grabbing its kitten by the scruff of the neck and running off with it to safety. The auction was about to begin.

'What exactly do you want me to say?' he asked.

'How art benefits humanity, all that kind of thing. Don't worry about it. How you look is more important than what you say. No-one will be listening, just watching. Sometimes no-one bids at all, and the auctioneer has to take bids off the wall. That's so embarrassing. But with you and me both here we should get a good price.'

Walter Wells, who was not accustomed to public speaking, demanded at least some prompting about the way in which art could serve humanity, and on the way to the plinth Lady Juliet told him to mention both the morality of aesthetics, and how suitable it was that the haves of the luxury trades – in which fine art was included – should do their bit for the have-nots. And perhaps a mention as to how she, Lady Juliet, had given her precious time freely, as the sitter.

'Wish me good luck,' he'd said to Grace as he went. But she hadn't replied, she was staring, along with everyone else, at a couple who had just come into the room. Even the string quartet faltered mid phrase. All eyes turned, as if to royalty, towards a good-looking older man in a very expensive suit – Walter had painted that particular Chairman of the Board type many a time, sitting behind some great burr-oak desk, or leaning up against a pillar at Company headquarters, dull, dull, dull – and a younger woman in a flame-coloured dress with a strong nose, a hard mouth, and a band of solid powerful gold around her neck; but who moved with a kind of focused energy, as if all the wind of the present, whirling around, had sought her out as its centre. Always hard to get on canvas, this kind of thing, this sense of the present made apparent, if only because those few whom fate so selected were seldom in repose. They never sat still.

7

Doris Dubois and Barley Salt found themselves at a loose end after their Caesar salad and sparkling water lunch at the Ivy. Barley had once been in the habit of ordering the fried fish and the thick chips and mushy peas but Doris had patted his tummy affectionately and said slenderness was youth, and a man as young at heart as he was should have a figure to go with it. It was remarkable how quickly rich and fatty foods began to seem gross; and the waist to return. He felt restless, though, as if serenity was situated somewhere in the fatty tissues, and only sexual pleasures with Doris seemed able to quell the feeling that something, somewhere, was not altogether right. It wasn't that he missed Grace: her fitful dry wit had come to seem like an evasion of real feeling; he felt reassured by Doris's earnestness and her appreciation of the higher things in life: if he missed Grace it was in the same way a young man gone off to college will miss his mother: he knows he must grow out of her, while occasionally hankering for the comforts of home.

But home, the mansion in which he and Grace had so casually lived, and had together lost all but passing interest in sex, was now, with Doris installed, a turmoil of builders, designers and security experts, too crowded by day for sex, and there was no point in going there until after seven, by which time most would have disappeared, but Doris had to be back in town by eight because she was going out live at ten. They decided to stay in town: Doris consulted her digital notepad and discovered an invitation to a charity auction at Lady Juliet's that evening.

'Lady Juliet!' said Barley. 'What a pleasant woman. My ex-wife and I used to be on quite good terms with the Randoms. I haven't seen much of them since the divorce. He's in rare metal recovery. Buys up de-commissioned nuclear weapons and so on and extracts the titanium.'

'Preserving the natural wealth of the planet!' said Doris. 'Way to go!'

'I'm not sure that that's his prime motive,' said Barley, brutally. 'Quite a lot of Russians get exposed to quite a lot of radio-activity on the way.'

'Darling,' said Doris, 'you shouldn't be so cynical. It isn't nice. Shall we trot along? There's a party at the British Library Manuscripts Room, but they're so nervous there in case you spill champagne on the Book of Kells, or something, it's no fun. A charity auction in a private house might be quite entertaining, and it's always fascinating to see how other people live.' Doris wanted to be on good terms with the Randoms. If Grace could do it, so could she.

'They're quite dull, really,' said Barley, cautiously. 'They don't have many books in the house, but she's such a nice woman.'

Doris did not have anything to wear, so they went to South Molton Street by cab – Barley's chauffeur Ross had a sick mother – and were dropped off at the end of South Molton Street where they strolled along to Browns, and Barley watched while Doris bought a kind of silk slip dress by a Japanese designer, in yellow and orange and gold. Tall, slinky, reserved girls attended her – ladies in waiting – and he stood and watched with his hands in his pockets. Grace never in a million years would have wasted time and money in this way; he loved it, and said as much to Doris.

'Yes but then darling you must remember I am a perfect size ten and your ex-wife is a very imperfect size fourteen, probably sixteen, and women like that don't much go for shopping.' Doris would have been a size eight but the BBC insisted that she not be too thin. Programme presenters had to send the right message to the nation. Otherwise she would have had the plain salad not the Caesar salad, with its croutons and plentiful dressing, for lunch. The dress cost £600, and Barley paid. But Doris was selling her flat in Shepherd's Bush and insisted that she would pay the money back, in time. Being spoiled was wicked, but she liked her independence.

Afterwards they took a walk through Grosvenor Square, watching as some Japanese children chased pigeons till their mother called them away, then strolled on to Bond Street and the peaches and cream décor of Bulgari, where even more charming girls, and men too, showed them jewellery under strong lights, and they decided on a sleek modern piece, a necklace, stripes of white and yellow gold, but encasing three ancient coins, the mount following the irregular contours of the thin worn bronze, which somehow went perfectly with the Japanese dress, though out of such different cultures, and Barley paid £18,000 for it, and they took it away with them. Doris fell silent at this point about paying him back. But what was money for but to be spent? Barley had done very well when the Canary Wharf complex had been constructed. Taken a risk everyone (including Grace) said he shouldn't, and it had paid off, and these days money just made money. It mounted and mounted. Doris was like him, a risk taker. A stroll to Heywood Hill bookshop where Doris was on first name terms with the knowledgeable and courteous gentleman who ran it, to receive their recommendations for her *Out of the Past* clip, and then it was time for Lady Random's. They made every minute of the time they had: it was in both their natures – Grace tended to sit about dreamily doing nothing – and Barley did feel a little tired when they got to the stolid cream house with pillars. Caesar salad is not much to sustain a man accustomed all his life to fried fish and chips and peas, but he supposed the canapés at the Randoms' would be plentiful and nourishing: not everything can be low fat.

'My God,' said Doris, after she had changed and made her entrance; all expensive simplicity. 'I do believe that's your ex-wife over there. How on earth does she get into a do like this?' Lady Random in her niceness had let Doris change in her, Lady Random's dressing room, where Doris had much admired various bottles of scent, but kept quiet about the décor, which favoured Fauve, and looked to her rather too like the TV backdrop from which she presented her book reviews on the programme. Literature was considered a worthy subject, but the set design was calculated to liven things up as much as possible. The two women had a brief conversation before Lady Random tactfully left Doris alone to change, in which Lady Random said to Doris that she and Barley must come to dinner some time, and Doris had invited them down to Wild Oats (as she had re-named Barley's, and formerly Grace's manor house home in the country) for the August weekend, if they were not to be in the Bahamas. But there was something about Lady Random's attitude which annoyed Doris: Doris had been definite about dates: Lady Random had not. Doris felt she was snubbed and was not accustomed to it.

'Barley,' she said now, 'get your ex-wife out of this room or I can't stay in it. Fetch the police or something. She's a murderess.'

'Darling,' said Barley, waving across the room at Grace, 'she is murderous and a would be murderer, Judge Tobias agreed with you there, but she has done her time and I don't imagine she is going to attack you right here and now.'

'Hell hath no fury,' said Doris, but subsided for the time being, because a young man of extraordinary beauty was now standing in front of a portrait he had apparently painted. It was of Lady Juliet Random and it made her appear kind, beautiful, intelligent and serene, if in a slightly Rubensesque way. This was how Doris would have preferred to look: sometimes legs can be too long, faces too narrow, hair cuts too Princess-Di-ish for comfort. Too TV all round, in fact. The world might currently reckon Doris the hottest thing since microwaved jam, what with her new British-made millionaire husband, but Doris herself had her doubts. You could do so much with style and pizzazz and move so fast no-one had time to perceive the flaws, but Lady Juliet could still look good when calm and reposed. And she would never go out of fashion as Doris could, and Doris knew it. One day the world would sigh when they saw Doris on TV and say *not her again*. Doris must lay up treasure and self-confidence against that day.

Round Lady Juliet Random's firm and flawless painted neck was a rare, colourful Bulgari piece, a necklace in red gold and steel, bright porcelain and deep ruby, and Doris knew she must have it. She and Barley had seen one like it, but not quite like it, in the Bulgari store that afternoon: and decided against it, and chosen instead the one she now wore round her neck, a piece not so vivid, perhaps, more muted, more somehow *now*, for what were Barley and Doris but *now*. It had been a fraction of the price, moreover, £18,000 not £275,000, and Doris sincerely hoped that this factor had not entered Barley's judgement. She had been talking about paying him back, of course, but he surely realised this was not really on the cards. She was a working girl, he was a wealthy man, and he loved her and must prove it. There was nothing she hated more than a mean man. She loved the necklace she had on, with its ancient Roman coins and its contemporary Roman flair, of course she did, it was just that now she wanted Lady Juliet's as well.

In fact she could not remember wanting anything so much since the time twenty years ago when her father Andrew the jobbing builder from Yugoslavia had bought her mother Marjorie the waitress a diamond ring from Ratners, to celebrate their wedding anniversary. That had been on Doris Zoac's thirteenth birthday. Her father had married her mother just in time for the birth: in fact it had been as Marjorie said 'I will' that she had gone into labour. Or so the family story went. So Doris felt very much part of the marriage, and had somehow craved a diamond ring as well, but had been given only a dressing-table in horrid orange plastic to celebrate; in effect shut out, sent back to her room. We all have our problems.

The auction had started. She pulled Barley's arm.
'Barley,' she said, 'I want that necklace. The one in the painting.' He felt a tremor of annoyance, much as he loved her. Want, want, want! He remembered what his mother used to say to him when he was a child, and had wanted a pair of shoes which didn't let water, or a piece of bread before he went to school. '*Then want must be your master.*'

*   *   *

33

Grace at least had understood poverty: she had never experienced it herself, of course: she was the daughter, the eldest of three, of a Harley Street doctor of good family. She had never gone hungry, never known physical hardship, the pinch of cold or the wet shoes that must be worn because there are no others. Her parents had been good and kind, if unimaginative. They had liked Barley well enough when she brought him home, and he had given them an opportunity to congratulate themselves on their lack of snobbishness. They had admired his looks, his drive and his energy, but he was not quite what they had wanted in a husband for Grace. They were vague enough about exactly what it was that they did want – *'all we want is for you to be happy'* – but they had expected the source of her happiness to be someone with a title or at least a good accent. They had brought their daughters up to have social consciences: now perhaps they saw the consequences of their actions. Children have a way of listening to what their parents say and taking it at face value, not noticing the subtext. Spout egalitarian principle and the young take it to heart. When not at their boarding schools the girls would vie with one another as to who in the holidays could work with the most deprived groups in society. Battered wives, disadvantaged children, dysfunctional estate families. All three had picked up boyfriends in the back streets, but only Grace had stayed the course.

'What these families need,' Barley would say during the days of their courtship, in the backs of cars and down alleyways, 'is not some middle-class girl telling them what's what, it's a sodding cheque for ten thousand pounds straight up.'

Be that as it may, he could see that Grace had still ended

up understanding more than Doris ever would about the tribulations life can bring. Doris believed everyone was like her, only with less talent and less money. She felt pity for no-one, except perhaps for size twelve girls, who could not get down to a size ten. She felt lust, and ambition, and happiness, and possibly love, but not charity. Yet Barley loved her and admired her for what she was: he loved the flattery of her attention, the way celebrity rubbed off like gold dust on all around. It was absorbing, a freedom from responsibility, it was no less than he deserved, and the only penalty had been hurting Grace, if Grace cared for him at all. In the long term he had done her a favour. She would be okay again within the year, everyone had told him so. She would get going, and rediscover herself and start a new life. She would flourish the way everyone said women did after their long-term husbands had gone. Marriage was not for life. Grace by her manner and demeanour had demonstrated that she meant to go early and gracefully into old age and he did not and that was that. Now she sat alone on the other side of the room with her strange familiar half smile, and seemed not to see him, and did not respond when he waved.

He had been with her to this very room some twenty times, he supposed, over the years: he had cleaved unto her, as it suggested in the marriage ceremony, but who could take all that stuff seriously any more? And now she was a stranger to him, a wave across a crowded room, and that, after all, was what he had set out to achieve. Grace seldom asked for anything: if he gave her money she would only send it to Carmichael in Australia, who was better off fighting his own way through the world, if fight was in him, which he doubted. But Carmichael had to be given a chance.

And then Grace had gone and spoiled what he had planned as an amicable divorce and tried to run down Doris Dubois, the great Doris Dubois, in a car park. He had gone to visit her in prison, which had caused a dreadful row with Doris, and then Grace had actually refused to see him.

As for Doris, he had spent just about twenty thousand pounds on her during the course of the day and now she was escalating her expectations tenfold. He had once set up a mistress in a nice little flat: it had been the same thing. Poppy had droned on and on about the central heating not working and asking for a better fridge and so forth, and he had got fed up with that; but this! Not £129 for a gas bill: you could put three noughts on the end of that, and double it.

'What do you expect me to do?' asked Barley. 'Go up to Lady Juliet and offer to buy it? Write her a cheque here and now and take it from her neck and put it round yours?'

'If you truly loved me that's exactly what you would do,' said Doris, but she had the grace to giggle. 'At the very least you could put some pressure on that dreadful little fat man she's married to, to make her do it. He's some sort of business associate of yours, isn't he? He won't want to piss you off, not the great Barley Salt.'

'Tell you what,' said Barley, who wanted to concentrate on the auction – bidding had started at £8000, and was moving upwards by £200 increases. The young artist was looking startled and gratified and was smiling his excitement over at Grace, for some reason. 'I'll buy you the painting instead.' And he joined in the bidding.

Doris jumped up and down with irritation.

'But I don't want the painting,' she said. 'I want a real Bulgari necklace with a bit of colour in it. Why would I want to hang a painting of another woman in my house? She's at least a

36

size fourteen, it would be bad luck. Besides, I've just gone to all this expense and trouble with Wild Oats for your sake, and it's just not the right place for paintings. Yes: half sheep in aspic. No: stuff in a frame flat on a wall. That poor sweet young artist, no wonder no-one takes him seriously.'

Hang it all, thought Barley, *she'd* gone to the expense? *I've* gone to the expense, and if I want a painting I'll bloody well have one, and hang it on the wall – and carried right on bidding.

'Twelve thousand five hundred,' offered Barley.

'A man with excellent taste,' quipped the auctioneer. He was a well-known actor who did a lot for charity, and his voice boomed goodwill and bonhomie.

'Thirteen thousand,' said a man whom Barley recognised as a colleague of Sir Ronald's, Billyboy Justice from South Africa. Now why? Charity? Perhaps. More likely to be brown-nosing Sir Ronald, and thinking this was the way to do it, through his wife. Probably after a government contract of some kind. Sir Ronald had close links with Downing Street. Justice had an interest in lewisite, a fast acting version of mustard gas, now in active de-commission worldwide, at least theoretically, and leaving out Baghdad, as usual. Thanks to new advances in the technology applicable to the disposal of chemical weapons, high quality pure arsenic could now be obtained from the treated gas, and sold at a good profit to the gas manufacturers worldwide. It was a good new business if you had the nerve for it, and Sir Ronald was fast moving out of nuclear recycling into chemical, as the great powers agreed to dispose of at least some of their arsenals, to make way, no doubt, for new.

'Thirteen thousand five hundred,' said Barley.

Oh well, thought Doris, if he wants to be such an idiot, let

37

him. She could always put Lady Juliet in her Shepherd's Bush flat, which she had more or less decided not to sell after all. She needed a good *pied-à-terre*, look at what had happened today, too far to go back home, and not all that cosy when you got there; and still with the stuffy if non-corporeal presence of Barley's ex-wife around – it somehow seemed to have got into the wooden floors of Wild Oats. She should have had them all taken up, and not drawn back at the last moment, fearful of yet more dust and disarray. How could the living hang around haunting the way Grace did? '*This place is mine by order of precedence.*' Like the Maoris claiming New Zealand and the Aboriginals Australia and the Palestinians, Israel. '*We were here first.*'

It was nonsense of course, yet oddly persuasive. Doris herself had a Mother Courage turn of mind. The land belongs to those who till it. The children belong to those who look after them. The house belongs to those who love it. Yet what had Grace ever done for Wild Oats except let the mice take over and the Agas rust, and not touch the plumbing since the day she moved in, back in eighty something.

Perhaps Barley would have her portrait painted: if the young painter – Walter Wells – came to the flat she could just about afford the time, find a window or two in her busy diary, at least it was only round the corner from work. Just to sit and be, and be appreciated. The more she thought about it, the better a deal keeping her flat seemed. Lady Juliet could be moved to the bathroom, her own portrait could take pride of place in the living room, which heaven knows had seemed attractive enough until Barley came along and dangled Wild Oats under her nose. And she needed a night or so alone from time to time. Sex with Barley was quite exhausting: it wasn't exactly the price you had to pay with a new man, because in all fairness she enjoyed it too, but it was tiring if you were trying to run an arts programme as well.

'Fourteen thousand,' said Sir Ronald's colleague, Billyboy Justice

'Good Lord,' came Lady Juliet's laughing, charming voice, 'fancy being worth so much! You're all such flatterers.'

'I don't know what's in it for Barley Salt,' said Sir Ronald sotto voce to his wife, 'but if that peasant Justice thinks I'm doing him any favours because he's buying you for his bedroom wall he's very mistaken.' Sir Ronald loved Lady Juliet. Everybody seemed to love Lady Juliet, that was the trouble. She was so used to adoration she couldn't tell a come-on from a chat. He had named a range of landmines after her, in those bad old savage days when there was more money in making arms than in taking the things to bits.

'Fifteen thousand,' said Barley.

'You're so sweet to me, Barley,' said Doris, thinking of other things.

'Sixteen thousand,' said Billyboy. He had started life as a chemist. His face had been burned in an explosion when he had been about to show a Defence Minister around his plant in Utah. The ecologists had got their knickers in a twist about saran emissions; the de-commissioning work itself was a simple enough process: you just cut up the weapons in a masher and then stewed them in water at forty degrees and most of the chemicals decomposed, or would were it not for the conventional propellants and explosives intrinsic to the weapons. It was these which could all too easily recombine in hot water and simply and old-fashionedly go off. Fortunately none of the Minister's party had been injured – and the contract had gone through. But for its renewal it needed a firm lobbying hand in parliament, which Sir Ronald could provide.

'Seventeen thousand,' said a squat man who had come to stand next to Billyboy. A Russian accent.

Barley turned to Lady Juliet.

'Who's the commissar?' he asked.

'Billyboy brought him along. Makarov, I think his name is. He looks a bit fierce, the way these men from Moscow do, but he's a real charmer. But then I love anyone who puts the bidding up.'

'Eighteen,' called out Barley.

'That's the way to go!' cried the auctioneer. 'Any advance on eighteen?'

'Twenty,' said a voice from the back and everyone turned to look at Grace, who blushed.

8

When Walter Wells went up on the little stage to say a few words about the role of art in eradicating world poverty he looked absurdly young and pretty. It was hard for anyone to take him seriously. He looked neither sufficiently corrupt for a young artist nor world weary enough for an old. He was badly in need of gravitas, thought Grace, but no doubt the passage of time would both bless and curse him with it. *If youth but knew, if age but could . . .*

Grace had assumed that Walter Wells was gay. He reminded her of her son Carmichael, now in Sydney whence he had fled from Barley. Lustrous black curls, narrow and Greek-God-ish face, lissom build, soft voice, intolerably handsome, dressed in shades and textures of black. Polo-necked black silk sweater, a waistcoat in thick, black cotton, black denim jeans; Carmichael had once told Grace all black hues were different, there was no such thing as true black; and she had been noticing this phenomenon ever since. In Walter Wells' case, unlike Carmichael's, as she was to discover, the layered effect was achieved with neither effort nor design by simply putting all garments through the washing machine at whatever temperature the dial happened to be pointing at. But then Walter was an artist, and Carmichael was a dress designer.

Grace's psychotherapist, Dr Jamie Doom, had told her that she should 'let Carmichael go'. That he had his own life to live, and had chosen wisely in going to Australia to do it, far away from his domineering father. He was not convinced by Grace's assertion that Carmichael – christened John Carmichael Salt, he preferred to use the middle name – had assiduously developed first his stammer and then his gayness in order to annoy Barley. Grace, he said, was being unrealistic in her disappointment – that Carmichael hadn't flown back to intervene and take his mother's side when Doris first appeared over the domestic horizon. She was unreasonable to hope he'd be in Court to give moral support – 'not even there to watch me being sent down!' No doubt, said Dr Jamie Doom, from the sound of it Carmichael had his own pressing emotional problems in Sydney: perhaps, when it came to his parents, he wished a plague on both their houses. As it were.

Sometimes she suspected Dr Doom was in Barley's pay.

As for the Manor House, where she and Barley had spent so many good years, Jamie Doom could not seem to understand why the thought of Doris Dubois changing its name to Wild Oats and tearing it to bits so upset her.
'You told me you didn't like the place,' he said. 'Too big, too gloomy and too ostentatious.'

A hundred acres and peacocks which kept them awake at night, built by an 1860 version of Barley, who had made his money in railways, and tried to design it himself, all dark panelling and echoey plumbing. They'd moved in when Carmichael was six: when Barley made his first million. She'd wanted to stay where she was, with Carmichael at the local school, friends with other parents, a small garden to record the passage of the seasons, the familiar and the safe, down-market according to her parents' looks when they came to visit, but fine by Grace. But how Barley wanted to take the look off their faces. If he thought he'd do it by moving the family into the Manor House he was mistaken.

'A little ostentatious, darling,' they had said. 'But if you like it . . .'

And then there'd been the matter of the two Rolls-Royces. Grace had begged Barley not to, but nothing would stop him. In the year Carmichael was born both her sisters married: Emily to an estate manager in Yorkshire, Sara to a stockbroker in Sussex. Both had big weddings. Barley insisted on arriving in a hired Rolls: it was money they could hardly afford at the time. Grace had assured her husband that there were other ways of demonstrating his worth – surely her evident happiness was enough to keep her parents in their place, just about. But he wanted to impress, to sweep away their doubts, as he swept away hers.

When she first took him home the McNabs had taken him for a man of no education, some kind of building labourer. Within three months of his marriage to their daughter he'd been site foreman, within a year at business school, working and saving while Grace worked in a dress shop to pay the bills – a job at which she'd been spectacularly bad – and then into property, and able to buy two Rolls-Royces. But it was never enough for her parents, and could never be enough for Barley. Only Doris Dubois would turn out to be that.

Barley's first crash came when Carmichael was nine. The bottom suddenly fell out of the property market. The millions vanished. He had prudently put the Manor House into Grace's name, and the two Rolls-Royces too. Emily and Sara's husbands had invested heavily in Barley's business. They lost all they had too, including their houses. Grace wanted to sell the Manor House and share what there was. But Barley was against it.

'Of course he would be,' said Dr Doom, hearing the story. 'You had to have somewhere to live. Others must be responsible for their own lives.' If the Court hadn't made going to therapy a condition of her freedom she would have got up and walked out there and then.

'But the cars,' she said.

'What about the cars?'

'Nobody needs two Rolls-Royces in the drive,' she said. 'It's not as if I could drive. I wanted to sell them to help Emily and Sara, but he wouldn't hear of it.'

'Quite right,' said Dr Doom. 'The resale value of those cars is absurd.'

It was what Barley had said at the time. Since her prison sentence it had sometimes seemed to Grace that all men were the same man. It had certainly been the view of men enjoyed by most of her fellow inmates. They tended to have husbands and lovers who got drunk and beat them about, whom they wouldn't leave because they loved them, but were nevertheless seldom inclined to speak well of men in general.

Sometimes, lately, Grace had felt nostalgia for prison. At least the place was well-peopled, albeit with a class of people to whom she wasn't accustomed. She had even made a friend: Ethel, a bookmaker who had run off with her employer's takings and earned three years for her pains. Ethel would be coming out in a couple of months; then Grace would find out how good a friend she was. Ethel might prefer to put the past behind her and Grace would understand it if she did.

Her own family had chosen to put any past which included her behind them, and she could understand that too. By the time Barley was declared bankrupt Grace's sisters were not speaking to her, and her parents barely so. They felt not only justified in their initial suspicions of their eldest daughter's husband, but that she had been tainted by him in some way. Nor did his return to prosperity impress them. They none of them came to visit her in jail. They'd felt they had put up with enough already when they opened the *Telegraph* one morning to find Grace's picture staring back at them, portrayed as an aggrieved and murderous wife. She had only herself to blame.

9

Grace had been out of society for so long, embroiled in a divorce, a court case, a prison sentence, then the shock of the new in her gloomy, lonely apartment, that she easily misjudged what was going on around her. Even leaving Carmichael out of it, it was not surprising that she assumed Walter Wells was gay. It had become the tactic of many perfectly heterosexual young men to affect a misleading campness as if in self-defence: a softness of voice, a delicacy of movement, an all-pervasive irony of gesture. This they did to obviate the anticipated reaction of so many young women they approached. '*Don't you lay hands on me, you rude, crude, heterosexual beast, you macho scum, all sex is rape, stop looking at me in that disgusting way, you're harassing me, stalking me, go away!*' To take on the colours of gayness was to be given time and space to charm and flirt their way in, as Walter Wells now did into Grace Salt's comprehension. She did not turn her head away: she recognised a fellow victim, a young man who might be Carmichael, someone with whom the world was not fully at ease, and so she consented to smile and talk to him, and have fellow feeling with him, and not turn her head stiffly away. '*We both know how to suffer.*'

It was true she had wondered where exactly Walter Wells' self-interest lay. She was not naïve. She was well aware that beautiful and fashionable young men do not talk to unfashionable women and flatter them unless there is some deeper agenda at work. They do not sit smiling and chatting out of sheer goodness of heart, not to a depressed woman of a certain age, wearing an old dress found in the bottom of a suitcase snatched from home in her hurry to leave, a dress she wore on her honeymoon. (A shake and a cloud of dust and it had seemed to Grace as fit to wear as anything ever would.) But what could the agenda be? She did not look rich or important. She was not hung with jewels. She did not look like the kind of person who would commission a painting of herself, sitting as she did lonely and neglected in a corner, trying to be invisible. And besides, men did that: husbands, fathers, lovers, the kind of men Grace now, perforce, did without. Perhaps she reminded him of his mother? She decided that was it. He was a young man of charm and talent, lucky enough to have Lady Juliet's sponsorship and attention, but he was sensitive and edgy, the artist amongst patrons, and insecure as befitted his age; and thus he had sought her out, dull and dowdy as she was.

When Barley had entered the room with Doris, flushed and pleased, and all conversation was stilled in acknowledgement of their presence, their celebrity status, Grace had felt what she later described as the 'thickening of the blood in her veins'. Doris saw her, but looked through her as if she did not exist; which was to be expected. But Barley saw her and waved, and in this gesture Grace read the end of all intimacy. He did not

47

even have the interest left to hate her. Her heart faltered; it could hardly get the blood round her body it was so sluggish, as if she'd gone out of a warm room into the sudden sharp and horrid cold of a blizzard. It was the cold of disappointment, the knowledge that Barley was gone from her forever. If it was not one painful truth which dawned in upon her, it was another.

How hard it was to rid herself of the feeling that Barley was somehow still on her side. That when the chips were down he would leave this room with her, not Doris, and the joke would be over. And then it would be her turn to play, and perhaps she would toss her head and say *no! who? you? who are you to me?* and go home with someone else. Or perhaps not. Barley had been to visit her in prison, but she had refused to see him. Some few powers prisoners do have, and this was one of them. Simply to snub. Except as the long hours dragged by, locked in her cell – so many staff were engaged in the attempt to forestall the passage of drugs by kiss, or embrace; to dampen down hysteria, or cart back the screaming, and the distracted and the lost-it to their quarters, that those without visitors must stay locked up – the spasm of pride had seemed mere folly. And now! Locked in her head, her body, her mouth smiling; while the few people who remembered she was there at all turned to see how Grace once Salt, now Grace McNab, reacted to the entrance of the noted celebrity lovers.

They mean to humiliate me with their happiness, was what she thought: Barley so smooth and well-suited, his teeth newly remade: Doris in the fabulous flame-coloured dress and the Bulgari necklace with the burnished coins set in heavy gold.

Only two years back and Barley had offered to buy Gracie, his then wife, just such a gift for her birthday, but she'd refused, having rung the shop to find out how much it cost. He'd taken it as a snub: he felt her resistance to what he was, obdurate in her preference of the stony past they had once shared over the soft comfort of the uneasy present. Somewhere she was still Grace McNab, not Gracie Salt, she was her parents' daughter. Dr McNab the Harley Street surgeon was well enough off, but what was left at lunch would be eaten for dinner: *waste not want not* filled the air as yesterday's cold sprouts were fried for breakfast. The faint smell of antiseptic from the surgery below, the bleakness of the high, cold waiting rooms with their polished furniture and harsh red Persian rugs, their neat copies of *Country Life*; the stoicism of dull patients, their pain and dereliction of the body so bravely borne – these things she took to be ordinary; the base from which all other conditions departed.

Forever she tried to re-create her childhood home: forever Barley tried to thwart her. Barley was in flight from the poverty of his; she longed to return to the careful respectability of hers. So much Dr Jamie Doom had taught her. It was her role to thwart Barley's wishes. She tried not to but she couldn't help it. The more Barley craved luxury and extravagance the more uneasy she felt; the more, to save his very soul, she would insist on cooking for his smart dinner guests herself and not get in expensive caterers – what was an Aga for, but to bake her own cheese straws for parties – murmuring that surely everyone appreciated home cooked food? And he'd grow pink and desperate in his new Jermyn Street finery, and she'd be in a dress from Marks and Sparks, Marble Arch. Of course he'd got fed up with her.

She should have done so much so differently, but how could she? She was the person she was. Other women seemed able to turn themselves into something they had not been born to – Doris Dubois had started life as Doris Zoac, and had honed herself into new shape – but that skill was beyond Grace. She had once turned from Gracie McNab to Grace Salt, and now she was turning back perforce and that was bad enough.

The money that should have been Carmichael's was going round Doris's neck and on a painting that was pleasant enough, but if the painter had only been paid £300 a week for painting it, as he'd assured her, why should it fetch so much? It didn't make sense.

'Up we go!' enthused the auctioneer whose face everyone knew but whose name no-one could remember. 'Any advance on eighteen thousand?'
'Twenty,' Grace said, before she could stop herself, and then felt insecure because all faces turned towards her and so she blushed.

10

Walter Wells was gratified. Grace Salt wanted to buy his portrait of Lady Juliet, and for such a sum! It occurred to him that she must have money to spare and that was no bad thing because he was certainly short of it.

Lady Juliet had jumped up and down with pleasure when Barley Salt came in and said 'Now we'll see some real action. But if they meant to come why didn't they say so, and I wouldn't have asked Grace. How embarrassing!' Apparently the telly diva Doris Dubois – for Walter recognised her: her programme which had started with a book bias was increasingly casting its eye over the visual arts – was his new wife in place of Grace. He could see the attraction – he would quite like to paint her, he thought: the definitions of her outline were interestingly hard, sharp and clear: most people tended towards such fuzziness of being it was hard to tell where the edges were. His attention drifted towards Barley Salt, who had come into the bidding as well; he and the wonderfully louche South African, Billyboy Justice, were fighting it out.

*   *   *

'Twenty thousand,' said Grace. Walter turned to look at her; blushing, he saw, from nerves?

'How disgusting,' said Doris Dubois, rather loud and clear. 'That must be a hot flush. Can't she even take hormones?'

The bidding stopped, as if having startled itself out of existence.

The hammer fell.

'Sold to Mrs Salt,' said the actor-auctioneer, who had dined at the Manor House once or twice in the old days, and clicked that he recognised his one-time hostess. He remembered her with affection. She would serve prawn cocktails followed with steak-and-kidney pie when you were grimly resigned to another dose of sun-dried tomatoes, rocket salad, and seared tuna.

'I'm Mrs Salt,' said Doris Dubois.

'My name is Grace McNab,' said Grace, firmly.

'I'm sorry,' said the actor-auctioneer, confused, but everyone makes mistakes, and it wasn't as if he was being paid for this. 'Sold to the lady in the red velvet dress.'

Walter Wells heard Barley Salt say to Grace, 'You can't afford it, Gracie. You'll have to touch your capital. Let me do it.'

He heard Grace say, 'No. If I have to live my own life not ours I'll live it my way. Go away.' Walter knew then he would have a hard time wresting her emotions away from Barley and towards himself; but he also knew he meant to do it.

'Please can we go now, Barley,' said Doris Dubois. 'I really can't waste any more time.'

'Why, Doris,' said Grace – McNab or Salt? – sweetly, 'the price tag is still on your dress.' And so it was, saw Walter, a much bar-coded card hanging out the almost-collar at the back of the orange silk. Doris was a rose unfurled and bright, not blown, like Grace: the kind his mother sometimes bought at Woolworth's. 'To add colour,' she'd say. 'Cheap but cheerful – they've had such a struggle against odds to live, they sometimes do it very well.'

Doris Dubois turned to Grace and said 'Bitch!' rather loudly. 'Oh come on now,' hissed Barley, 'Don't let's have a scene. Can't we all settle down and be friends?'

'Are you joking?' asked Doris Dubois.

'Are you mad?' asked Grace McNab.

Lady Juliet trotted up decorously with some nail scissors, and said reproachfully: 'Poor Grace was only trying to be helpful.' And in full view of all the room – plus a camera crew which had just happened to stop by for the *London Nite* programme – she snipped off the tag, while Doris stood furious and tried to laugh it off, saying: 'Six hundred pounds! The Little Children, Everywhere could do with that – as worn by Doris Dubois.'

'She's not stripping off in public,' said Barley, 'but it's okay by me. Sell away!'

So Doris Dubois went upstairs spitting and fuming to change into jeans and an *LC,E* T-shirt someone conjured up, and put her dress up for auction. In one way she was pleased: it was what Hollywood stars did, and suggested that the magic of her fame was being properly acknowledged. But she didn't want to lose the dress her Bulgari necklace had been chosen to match; nor did she like the way Barley had leapt to his ex-wife's defence; least of all did she like how Lady Juliet had strong-armed her – albeit in the interests of Little Children, Everywhere, whose needs must be respected, certainly in public. Not that Doris liked children, anywhere, one bit. But there were too many witnesses for her to be able to defy Lady Juliet safely. She would have her revenge.

11

Once I had bought the painting I didn't know what to do with it. I wrote a cheque for it, and filled out the stub, and felt quite proud of myself. For years I'd left that kind of thing to Barley. The painting was taller than me and twice as wide. The frame was gilded, and so heavy I wasn't going to be able to lift it and tuck the thing under my arm. With Lady Juliet's smile glimmering above it, the Bulgari necklace shimmered with ruby light, and the image seemed a miraculous object, like a Byzantine icon that was about to bring so much benefit to everyone. The money would go to Little Children, Everywhere and here I was, in possession of the concentrated essence of so much time and skill: the very soul of Lady Juliet distilled onto canvas. Walter Wells was also very good at the texture of fabric and the glittery depth of precious stones. I liked it that he was. More, I had answered Doris Dubois back. I might yet do more of it. And Barley had shown concern for me. I was elated.

Which was how Doris Dubois ended up selling her new dress at a charity auction and it was on TV that night, with her wearing T-shirt and jeans and frankly looking a trifle odd in the ornate company she was keeping. She would have put me in prison for the rest of my life if she could have. The dress fetched £3250, having gone up in jumps of £250 and nice Lady Juliet was very grateful, and so no doubt were the Little Children, Everywhere. But Doris was not grateful to me at all. These victories were small and silly but they were victories. And nothing as to what was to come.

'Can I help you with that?' asked the young painter, startling me. His eyes were so bright and attentive. Once, I remembered, many men had looked at me like that. But after you have been married for a while they stop, and you forget. Perhaps a certain kind of woman catches the essence of man in marriage: the female body picks up the smell and texture of the partner if only as a consequence of so much physical contact, so much acceptance and absorption of what are tactfully called body fluids. In these days of safe sex I daresay it doesn't happen so much. But here I was, all that reversed, stopped, my own separate self emerging, seventeen-year-old Dorothy McNab again: no longer Dorothy Salt. I had slept and now I had woken, to find three decades and more had passed, and here was a young man gazing at me as if I were an object of delight.

'Well yes you can help,' I said. 'I was going to take it home in a black cab, but I don't know whether it will fit inside, or how I will hang it on the wall once I'm home.'

'Oh it will fit,' he said. 'It will fit very well. We could take it back to my place and hang it on my wall.'

'It would seem more appropriate to hang it on mine,' I said, 'since I have paid so much for it. One is expected to get the value, surely?'

'Move in with me,' he said, 'and let us get the value together. We can turn Lady Juliet's face to the wall, we can stack her amongst the landscapes, when we want our privacy, which I imagine will be often.'

We went back to his place together in his van, he hung Lady Juliet on the wall and I stayed to get the value of it. And I had thought he was gay.

12

'It is too bad,' said Doris Dubois, 'that your bitch of an ex-wife should own a painting which is mine by rights.' Their sheets were pink satin – as chosen by Paul the designer – but Doris didn't think they were truly satisfactory. Sex in satin sheets was fine in principle but crap in practice. They were cool when you first laid your head on them but too soon got hot and clammy, and worse, slippery, putting her in mind of the cod-liver oil her mother Marjorie Zoac had made her daughter take every morning.

'Now there's nothing for it, darling – unless you get me the real necklace from that other bitch, Lady Juliet.'

'It's not as we had any use for the painting,' said Barley. 'As you pointed out yourself, it wouldn't have fitted in here at all. My ex-wife should have had her portrait done when I asked her, seven years ago, back in the old days, when a wall was a wall and had a picture rail.'

'More fool you bidding for it, then.' She was in a bad mood. Barley seldom got the brunt of it – she reserved this for the camera crew and occasionally some literary guest or other on her book show. She had once reduced a young writer to tears on live TV by describing her sensitive novel as a load of self-pitying crap. It had done wonders for sales, as she had pointed out to the hundreds who wrote and phoned and e-mailed – e-mail could be a terrible burden: so much instant communication – in protest. And somebody had to keep the flame of literary criticism alive.

'I liked the look of that young painter,' said Doris, more to feel the sudden tautness of Barley's body beside her than because she did. 'I suppose you fancied him,' said Barley, hurt to the quick. A pang to the heart that felt almost physical. Grace had never hurt him like this. But that only proved his relationship with Grace had never been truly intense; more like a cosy kind of friendship. Love hurt, everyone knew.

Doris had remarked that Grace really looked her age all of a sudden, in that dreadful old dress, and it was true enough. He remembered her wearing that particular outfit once to a rather important dinner party; something to do with Carmichael, when Carmichael was small and used to embarrass everyone by coming down to family dinner in a dress. If he'd been allowed to punish Carmichael there and then he might have knocked some of the cissy nonsense out of him, but the therapists had been brought in and that was the end of that. He could not forgive Grace for the way she had colluded, for what she had in effect done to his son: stripped him of his manhood. He couldn't say so to Doris, of course: any mention of Carmichael was met by sulks and stares, almost worse than when he referred to Grace. She wanted him to have started his life the day he met her. He remembered those dinners; Grace would never bring in the professionals, and insisted on doing the cooking herself, and hovering over tables of smart and useful people, sweaty and busy and nervous. Doris knew how to make the most of these occasions.

*   *   *

What a struggle it had all been: how wonderful it was to be shot of her, to have Wild Oats made what it ought to be, could always have been, were it not for Grace's obstructionist ways. They were a power couple, he and Doris, and their background should reflect it, and Doris was making sure that it would. He shuddered sometimes at the bills and was sure the contractors Doris used were ripping him off, but she assured him that £200,000 for a carpet for the hall and stairs was nothing these days. And that was just the carpets. The trouble was, his mind was on a bigger game. All things depended at the moment on a make or break deal in Edinburgh: a new opera house development with a major art gallery attached – the Opera Noughtie it was to be called, a major celebration of the first ten years of the Government's *Century in the Arts* project – and a worldwide-web tie-in. It was falling nicely into his lap, and being with Doris certainly helped. The deal was now a ninety-nine per cent certainty and would bring him in almost a billion, no worries. If it didn't, if the one per cent won through, he'd be skint – he'd need a lot more than a couple of hundred thousand to get him straight again. But he was on a lucky streak: meeting Doris, falling in love, actually marrying her, having her in his bed nightly and by rights – how could anything go better? When the house was finished, the drain on the purse would be over.

He could almost hear Grace's voice saying, 'What do you mean, when the house is finished? It was finished in 1865.' Doris was right, Grace could be as bitchy as the rest of them. Now Doris's hand was roving, her fingers tugging ever so gently at the hairs on his chest. She gave each of his nipples a quick kiss. Grace never paid him this sort of attention in the morning.
'Of course I didn't fancy him,' said Doris. 'Why, do you want

me to? Are you after a threesome? You, me and him. One has to be careful in case the press gets a hint, of course, but if that's what you want.'

Barley was shocked.

'Of course that's not what I want,' he said.

'I was only teasing, darling,' she was quick to reply. 'Some men do like that kind of thing, you'd be surprised.'

'Two girls and one man,' said Barley, 'I can see the point of that, but why would any man want another man?'

'If he truly loved his wife he might,' said Doris. 'If for example he was rather old and she was rather young and he couldn't satisfy her but still wanted to be involved. Why then he might make the sacrifice.'

'You're not suggesting,' said Barley, who had, he supposed satisfied his new wife twice that night already, 'that this applies to me?'

Doris laughed merrily, and tugged his chest hair some more. It was going a little grey and wiry.

'If there was the slightest suggestion of that,' she said, sounding quite offended, 'I would hardly have brought the subject up. I don't suppose I'd even be with you. Don't worry about it, you're better than most men of your age.'

Some questions, Barley had learned, it is better not to ask, in case you don't like the reply. Doris had of her own declaration slept with her boss on several occasions but that had only, she assured him, been to get her own programme. And when she had been a student there had been several forays into experiment with other students but that was only to be expected these days. He thought he would probably kill anyone she dared look at now. Grace had last been seen leaving the Sir Ronalds' with the painting plus the artist in an old van: so Ross the chauffeur had heard on the grapevine. Barley had not told Doris that; it would complicate his life too much.

He doubted he'd ever get to be Sir Barley now, not after the episode of Grace in the car park. But you never knew. The public had short memories; think of the Prince and Camilla.

'But darling,' Doris said now, her hand wandering down and patting his tummy, 'I do think we have to work a little harder at the gym to get the extra pound or so off. Nothing that ages a man so much as a beer belly.'

This was ridiculous; Barley had no beer belly. A beer belly was when you looked down and couldn't see your knees, and he was nowhere near as bad as that. He could perfectly well see his knees when he looked down: he was sure it was more than Sir Ronald could do, and certainly more than Billyboy Justice could. He wondered if he should move over into arms de-commissioning rather than property: but it was dangerous work, not just because of explosions, look at what had happened to Billyboy's face, but people in the field did tend to get folded into the trunks of cars, dead. He would stick to the world-wide-web, as his gesture towards global peace and understanding.

'I love you, darling,' said Doris Dubois, firmly replacing his hand, as it strayed, 'no matter what shape or size you are. It is you I adore, the one and only Barley Salt in all the world. Now if you're too bashful to make Lady Juliet a straight offer on her necklace, can we please stroll down to Bulgari tomorrow and see about them making me up one just like hers.'

'I don't think they'd do that, darling,' said Barley. 'I think they may have rules about exclusivity in commissioned work, things like that.'

'You're just too mean to buy it for me, darling. You're trying to get out of it.'

Well, she was right about that.

'In six months' time, Doris. If you can hang on for six months.'

'Anything can happen in six months,' she complained. 'The whole world can change.'

She was right about that too, but neither of them knew it at the time.

'I want that same young artist to paint me,' said Doris, 'If Sir Ronald can do that for his horrid Juliet, surely you can do it for me.'

'Yes, but Doris,' said Barley, 'you did say we couldn't have a traditional portrait in the new style Wild Oats.'

'*Yes but*,' complained Doris, 'how you do *yes but* me all the time. We'll make a concession and have just one room with a picture rail. The library, I think. Of course that means redoing the floors for an antique effect, and probably replacing the panelling, which will have to be restored because they made rather a mess of it taking it out, but it will be worth it.'

Her hand moved downwards. He gasped with pleasure.

'I don't want you to have a necklace too like Lady Juliet's,' he said. 'And I don't want a portrait too like hers, either. Does it have to be by what was his name, Walter Wells? Really I would prefer it if it wasn't.'

The hand retreated.

'What is this apparently peculiar business going on between you and Sir Ronald and the man with the odd name? Contracts and ministries and backhanders and all that?' She was keeping this one in reserve. He sighed. It was terrible how transparent others could be in their attempts to manipulate, and even more terrible how you simply accepted it, as you grew older and women grew younger.

'Doris,' said Barley Salt, as evenly as he could, 'there is no peculiar business going on. Everything is perfectly legal and above board with proper bills of sale approved by the Department of Trade. What makes you think otherwise?'

'Darling,' said Doris Dubois, patiently, 'there is always something going on. There are always other agendas. How else does the world go round? I'm not objecting, only remarking. I do have links with the environmental lobby, obviously. Good Lord, I even shared a bed with Dicey Railton for a couple of years. That was before he came out as gay, of course. Actually I always thought that was an affectation to help his political career. There was certainly no sign of it at the time. He was totally a completely charming and fantastic lover.'

This was the first Barley had heard of a relationship with Dicey Railton, who was a backbench MP, an embarrassment to the Government by virtue of the awkward questions he was so good at asking, especially when it came to matters of the arms trade and sanction breaking.

'I'd rather you weren't too close to Dicey Railton, Doris,' he said. 'You are my wife. We don't want the papers getting hold of it and nor do you.'

'True enough,' she said, regretfully. 'But this much is for sure, I don't intend doing Lady Juliet any favours. Not after she made me take my dress off and sell it. Does she hate me? Why did she ask your ex-wife to the same function as she asked us? Whose side is she on anyway?'

'I don't suppose you answered her invitation,' said Barley. 'And I wish you wouldn't think about it as a question of sides. This was meant to be a civilised divorce.'

'I never accept invitations,' said Doris, loftily. 'I just turn up or I don't. How does your ex-wife have the nerve to go out looking the way she does? Did she ever look in mirrors when she was with you? Or perhaps she found it in some charity shop. A charity dress for a charity auction, that's the way her mind would work. Poor darling, how you must have suffered. And you know she was famous through London for serving prawn cocktails?'

'What's wrong with a prawn cocktail?' He was baffled.

She laughed, her little high perfected trill. He adored it.

'Sweetheart, if you don't know I shan't tell you. Just leave it all to me and you'll have your knighthood in no time at all. It's absurd that Juliet gets to be a lady and I don't.'

There was a knock on the door. Barley had thought he had another half hour in bed with Doris, but it was the housekeeper to say the decorators had turned up and wanted to come in and measure up; and to his astonishment Doris got straight out of bed and let them in, not wanting to inconvenience them, she said.

Decaff coffee was served on the terrace, with grapefruit juice, which was rather acid for his stomach but he didn't like to say so, and low cholesterol croissants.

13

Walter Wells tells me he loves me. Walter Wells is much younger than I am. His body has a resilience mine does not. He bounds up the stairs to the studio we have shared for seven days; I go up them one at a time. He took me swimming to the local pool; he carves like a fish through the water; it parts only reluctantly for me. His body above mine is dark and sharply silhouetted as it moves with focused intent back and forth, back and forth. Mine is happy enough to receive this steady pounding, endless engine of desire, but feels surprised as if receiving what was not quite intended. I'm sure I never felt like this with Barley, who was always in rather a hurry, there was so much to be got on with. I can see that, though worldly wise I am really quite short of carnal knowledge: I daresay there are as many kinds of lovemaking as there are men. Who could I ask? If Ethel ever comes out of prison it is the kind of thing she might know. Walter Wells is still quite new to me; I am not quite sure yet what I can say or what I can't.

He smells of oil-paint and canvas, encrusted palettes and turpentine, cigarettes and McDonald's, where he eats Chicken

McNuggets with the sweet-and-sour dip, and of chlorine from the swimming pool, and there is some slight remembered flavour of Carmichael there when I held him against my breast, the smell of the baby boy pre-testosterone, don't ask me why. I love it all. All I regret is the decades without it, and if I had not been without it how could I have it now? Those in love are bats, quite bats.

Walter Wells's full name is Walter Winston Wells. www. We see some significance in this when really there is none, but then we see significance in everything. We suppose him to be a man of the future, and he laments that he can never catch up with me. He looks forward to being old, or so he says, to be able to turn into his father and be taken seriously. I tell him I think it is unlucky to wish old age upon himself, and he points out that it's a lot better than death. Both of us at the moment want to live forever and together.

The Indian summer is over and the nights draw in. It is cold in the studio so I wear winter woollies. Lady Juliet's painting has her face to the wall, in case she gets damaged, leaning up against a stack of canvases, mostly landscapes, a couple of still lifes. She is waiting merely for a wall space to become vacant. She can go up only when the next one is sold, he says. It would seem like favouritism, he says, to take down one already in place and so make way for Lady Juliet. Everything must take its turn, be done in due order. He has a very personal relationship with his paintings. If I were a different, younger, less patient person I could get quite jealous of them, he is so tender and thoughtful to them. I wonder if I should take the painting back to my flat and put it up, but we agree we like Lady Juliet and do not want her hanging there lonely in that desolate place. I have to go back sometimes for a change of clothes and a better bath than Walter can provide and to answer lawyers' letters and so forth, but I am always pleased to leave. It seems to me that every time I climb the four flights to the studio I do it more quickly and more easily. My feet have wings.

Walter reckons it will be only a couple of weeks before he sells a painting and Lady Juliet goes on the wall. He sells his paintings for less than a thousand pounds each. He has a gallery in Bloomsbury just round the corner from my mansion flat in Tavington Court, not far from the British Museum – coincidence! Coincidence! See how God has arranged everything for our benefit.

It is a feature of new love that the senses grow sharper, the eye grows brighter – even my poor tired ones, in their sixth decade of being, and all things have meaning. I did the Lottery and won £92. I suppose we are 'in love'. The public pool is more full of event and far more full of chlorine than my own ever was. Now Doris Dubois has doubled the size of the one at the Manor House, as Ross, Barley's chauffeur, tells me she has, it will be lonelier still. Good. But I hardly think of Doris Dubois these days and of Barley even less. Hate is minimally more powerful than love, it seems, certainly harder to lose from the system, or perhaps I never loved Barley; all he ever was, was habit.

I love Walter Winston Wells, www.iloveyou@studio.co.uknostop. The only cure for one man, as Ross pointed out, is another man. I met Ross by accident down at the swimming pool where Walter dove and I paddled. Ross was always an ally of mine: he knew what Barley could be like. Ross goes swimming to lose weight, and then goes straight to Kentucky Fries for a triple cheeseburger and baked potato with sour cream and chives. He reckons the sour cream is less fattening than butter. Ross believes what he wants to believe, and who doesn't? He's a great strong white-haired man with a loose jaw and big teeth, who used to be a security guard, and is now trained by Mercedes to get out of ambushes fast. Property is not the safest business in the world once you get to the top, especially now the Moscow Mafia have moved in. No such worries with Walter: I get on a bus.

Walter Winston Wells, www, was having trouble with his telephone bill, his rent, his council tax, the bill to his paint supplier – titanium white is a shocking price – and I paid them all. Good Lord, why should a man of talent be so burdened? He sells his paintings for between £500 and £900 – except for Lady Juliet which went for £20,000 – more like its true worth – and of course he didn't get a penny of that, Little Children, Everywhere, got it – unless the Randoms' embezzled it, which I don't suppose they did – and the Bloomsday Gallery takes sixty per cent and he is meant to give them everything he paints, because they once paid £400 of accumulated bills and he signed this wretched document. But of course he puts some aside and sells them privately. How else is he supposed to live? The Bloomsday is quite small and unfashionable, and Larry and Tommy who run it are weasly little creatures who speak through their noses and put VAT on the selling price including commission, so Walter has to pay more than his fair share. At least I think this is how it works – I can't quite get my head round it.

This morning I went swimming again and the waters opened up before me like the Dead Sea and I swam three lengths non-stop, easily. Walter made rather a meal of his normal five lengths and took a minute longer to complete the course than usual. But then we'd been at it all night. Five times, I think without a condom because of course we don't have to worry about having babies. This is my great regret, that I can't give him one; but I don't think he's worried. When I sat on the wooden bench in the cubicle to dry my feet it seemed to me that the flesh round my heels and the top edge of the soles was no longer purplish with broken veins but quite smooth and white. A little blue and sodden from the cold water – the heaters had broken down again, and as for the wave machine, forget it – but no more than that. Extraordinary what happiness can do. It speeds me up but slows Walter down, as if our bodies were seeking some kind of equilibrium of age. He is painting my portrait. I take that very kindly.

14

'Darling,' said Doris Dubois to Barley Salt, as they lay side by side in bed on a morning a little chillier than usual: the Indian summer was over: the trees in St James's Park had turned to gold, and the ducks fluffed out their feathers in the Round Pond, and Doris and Barley's London walks were brisker and shorter than they had been. They would get as far as the Albert Memorial, and admire its gilded glory, but before they reached Sloane Street Barley would suggest they turned back. 'Now what are we going to do about this necklace of mine?'

'We're going to wait,' said Barley Salt firmly, 'until various business affairs of mine are settled. Then you can have two.'

'A Bulgari necklace in the hand is worth two in the bush,' said Doris. 'I would really like one now and another one later. Who is to say what will happen in six months from now? You might have fallen out of love with me.'

'Never!' He could not contemplate that.

'My show might be taken off the air. There could be a palace revolution. Remember what happened to Vanessa Feltz.'

'You're the Queen of the ratings and Queen of my heart. No-one would dare.'

'There are straws in the wind. My dress should have made more than £3000. People just don't care any more. They're turning against me. Everything's going wrong. The ceiling fell down on our bed. An hour later and we would have been killed. We raved on air about *Grendel's Mother*,' – a new musical which had just bombed – 'and now the theatre's closing and what does that make me? A f***ing idiot, out of touch with public taste. And if Wanda Azim doesn't get the Booker for *Sister K* my name is going to be mud. We've really pushed that novel and it isn't honestly all that good – Dostoevsky did it better. My touch is slipping, darling, the magic's seeping out of everything.'

Doris was quite panicky, trembly, sitting up in bed. He'd noticed she got like this sometimes. She presented such a smooth and confident face to her public that only he, her intimate, her bed companion, knew what she went through; understood the tensions of the job and what she battled against.

'£3000 plus, for a dress that cost £600 an hour earlier isn't too bad a profit margin,' he consoled her. 'Five hundred per cent. Think about it, Doris. Just for having been in contact with your body.' His sums were swift and serviceable, and convincing at a meeting, if not necessarily accurate.

'The portrait of that cow Lady Juliet got at least twenty times its worth, and she's a nonentity. I know exactly what they paid the artist. I should have done better.'

'At least my ex-wife didn't buy the dress. You wouldn't have liked that.'

'She might have,' said Doris, frightened. 'If she can afford to buy paintings at charity auctions you're paying her far too much alimony. I want you to go to court and get it reduced.'

He tried to stroke her limbs into tranquillity, move her mouth into a smile, but she stayed quivery and anxious, tossing her head from side to side. She had taken cocaine the evening before. Only a little, she said, to give her courage and pizzazz for the show, she'd never take it recreationally, only for work, but how was he to know what was a little and what was a lot? He knew nothing about drugs. He needed to be in control of his circumstances at all times.

They were in bed in one of the guest rooms which was, miraculously, so far untouched by the decorators, and was much as Grace had left it; that is to say, full of soft chintz chairs, traditional rosewood furniture, and with flower paintings on the walls. They'd had to move out of the master bedroom a week earlier. The ceiling had fallen; a mass of old plaster and choking lime-dust had come tumbling down upon the bed and, bringing with it as it did a heavy new erotic central light fitting, sculpted in tangled wrought iron, designed by an Italian who normally made chocolate phalluses but who had lately turned her mind to art, had bent the bedstead altogether out of its expensive, elegant shape. The mattress could be salvaged, the bed itself could not. What was soft and pliant survived, as Barley pondered, what was rigid and determined seldom did.

He doubted that the insurance company would pay out for yet another claim. Already a leaking swimming pool, a collapse of the new garage into old iron workings underground, a hundred more minor mishaps Doris had insisted on claiming for, while he told her to wait for the biggie, warned her that it was a bad idea to waste goodwill on trivia. Now the biggie had happened. Something had gone wrong when the roof of the West Wing was being lifted six inches: incompetent workmen had let slip a heavy steel beam, which had crashed through a floor left for some reason almost without supporting beams. He had tried to suggest to Doris that they move to an hotel while work was completed, but she hated hotels. This was her home and she would not let Grace drive her out.

The last statement surprised him. What had Grace got to do with it? He had not imagined, especially after the murder attempt, that Doris felt even residual guilt about living in Grace's old house. A lot of things had gone wrong, but when you considered the mountain tribesmen Doris insisted on employing, through an extremely dubious building firm who got its workers free through a government work experience scheme, for some reason to do with her social conscience and her reputation with the public, it didn't require a curse from Grace to make things go wrong. Besides, he had reason to believe, from what Ross told him, that Grace was happy again. He was greatly relieved, if also surprised, to find himself acutely jealous. He had not expected this from himself.

He could not give in to pointless emotions. Life was essentially simple. Women failed to get to the top not because of male prejudice but because they refused to treat it as simple. They looked for emotional complications, and found them. Any male executive of forty had a wife and children at home. His female equivalent seldom did. Why? She'd wasted too much time and energy being female, preening and combing in front of mirrors, talking about her feelings, and five days out of every twenty-eight grasping her stomach and groaning. How did they expect to get to the top, let alone stay there? Not their fault, and certainly not man's: God's, if anyone's. Doris did not believe in God. We appeared on this earth, according to her, and then ran around a bit looking after oneself, and then winked out. And that was that. He, Barley, thought there was probably a bit more to it than that. Odd that Doris then had a concept of curses and he did not.

In the meantime, he, Barley Salt, could not afford to give way to unreasonable emotions such as sexual jealousy, added to the conviction that this Walter Wells was after Grace's money since he could not be after her body, Grace being past all that. Two mutually exclusive emotions. It would take up too much time trying to sort them out. He needed to focus his attention on the fact that Billyboy Justice and Co. were suddenly breathing down his neck over the Edinburgh site; they'd been caught mooting it about in government circles that it would do for some kind of chemical plant the government had to provide under international law, and quickly. Out of town, and on the estuary for contaminated shipping. He hadn't liked the fact that Billyboy had been at the Randoms'. Sir Ron put it about that Billyboy fancied Juliet, and that his heart bled for Little Children, Everywhere, but there was probably more to it than that. Government attitudes these days switched with the latest poll: they'd been pretty much static on environment-friendly and anti-industry issues lately, and pro-development – big high-profile developments, at any rate – but they could easily swing back to pro-science-and-industry policies, and any incipient arts complex might get scuppered.

The odds, once ninety-nine out of a hundred, were down to eighty. Not good at all. Not the kind of margin he felt safe with; he remembered the horrible meltdown when Carmichael was small and the house had had to go into Gracie's name. She'd given it back without a murmur. He couldn't quite see

Doris doing that. Not that there was going to be much house left, the way things were going.

In the meantime here was Doris quivering and moaning and weeping in his arms. He'd thrown in his life with Doris, he would see it through. That was that.

'It's my birthday next week,' she was moaning. 'You know how I hate birthdays. Everything going downhill, I bet you haven't even planned a celebration, not even a surprise party, why can't this horrible building work ever be finished, it's all Grace's fault, she never looked after a thing and God knows she never had anything to do, not like I have. What did she do all day? Eat, from the look of her. I hate this room, I want our proper bedroom back, you don't love me, why should you, I'm such a mess.'

'Our' bedroom made him feel happy. He was always pleased and gratified to be included in Doris's scheme of things. She was a Scorpio, full of charm, sexual charisma and spite. If she couldn't find anyone to sting she would sting herself to death, if need be. He'd worked with Scorpios in his time. They could make you go dancing to your own death.

Rashly, he asked her if she was pre-testosterone-menstrual. He knew she was, not that she let a little mess stand in the way of their pleasures. She fell upon him tooth and claw, as he had rather anticipated, and with Doris the boundaries between murder and sex were blurred. He was egged on to a powerful and determined sexual performance.

'We'll go to Bulgari tomorrow and buy the necklace,' he said. He was already exhausted, emotionally more than physically, and the day had only just begun.

'Why not today?' she was half joking, sunshine after squalls, fitful, trying to settle back into happiness. She was six years old sometimes. He was so moved by her, he gave in.
'Okay,' he agreed. 'Today.'

He'd manage it at lunchtime. He had been meeting Random at the club, but he'd cancel. He doubted it would tip any balances. And there was nothing more fun than shopping for jewels with Doris, knowledgeable as she was about fine stones, about almost everything, come to that; nothing more soothing than the soft-carpeted opulence of Bulgari, and the attentive staff, and the hushed reverence with which they attended to the whims of their customers, with that timeless and exquisite courtesy which has been offered the rich since society began. 'Then that's settled then,' said Doris. But she did add that if he was ever strapped for money she would of course give it back, and he could probably get what she wanted cheaper, if he was in the business of cheap, if he made an offer for the ruby and diamond necklace Lady Juliet had been wearing in the portrait. 'Because of course I can do all that Lady Juliet serene style too, if I want. Simple white dress, blonde hair on top and just the one spectacular piece. Not even earrings to match.' Did he think when she, Doris, wore the antique coin necklace with the matching earrings it was over the top? No? Good. And the conversation drifted back to how Wanda Azim had better win the Booker or her (Doris's) name would be mud in literary circles throughout the land.

And then: 'Put your arms round me,' she said, and they snuggled together happily for a bit, all passion spent; and she met him at Bulgari that lunchtime. On the way through the park, under the gilded spire of the Albert Memorial, with its writhing caryatids and pale bosomy imperial ladies, she kissed him and said what she really wanted for her birthday was a portrait of herself by Walter Wells. There, a bargain! One Bulgari necklace and one painting by Walter Wells would cost less than the two Bulgari necklaces he had promised her.

He said he'd think about it, but his mind was on other things: he'd just seen Billyboy Justice at the wheel of his own limo negotiating the new unexpected humps in the road opposite the Serpentine Gallery, and sitting next to him the Russian who had been at Lady Juliet's for the auction. Barley knew, he just knew, that Billyboy was going to lunch with Sir Ronald Random, and they'd be talking about how the country needed a greater industrial base if it was to hold its own in the new Europe, and Art might be the part of the great way forward for France but it was not for Britain. And Sir Ronald Random, having been stood up by Barley at such short notice, might be paying more attention than he normally would.

It didn't help that Lady Juliet seemed fond of Grace, or she wouldn't have been asked to the auction. People, even in this day and age, did still seem to take sides. It had seemed such a simple idea at the time, to divorce Grace and marry Doris, and no-one's business but their own.

He'd been wrong, and he was not accustomed to being wrong.

15

Walter Wells loves me. At night his hands explore my body, and it doesn't even occur to me that he will find fault with any part of me. After years of sleeping with Barley and worrying if my tummy is too fat, am I doing the right thing, should I just lie here or should I involve myself more? His strong cool fingers move over my thigh, my back, over all my warm being, my smaller rounded compact self enclosed in his long bony self. How naked men and women complement each other in a bed: him hard, her soft, all that yin and yang stuff. So much pleasure! He pinches my flesh between finger and thumb, as if to prove it's real, that he's not dreaming. Yet this body of mine is all imperfection; by what magic is he so deluded? What was once smooth and resilient is now dry to the touch, and flabbier, so unfamiliar to me when my own fingers encounter it, it could belong to a stranger, a third in the bed.

Walter Wells sees no ugliness in this. 'I love you,' he says. 'You are so beautiful.'
'You think I am,' I protest. 'You know I'm not really. Everything looks better when it's young, and I'm not young.'

But he likes the blown rose not the bud, he tells me so. The bud is full of expectation that must end; there's so much sorrow and disappointment held up in store.

I look at myself in the mirror and I see certain changes I can't quite believe. My eyes begin to brighten. I would think I was growing young again, that nature had reversed its processes, that God had relented in his dire and doomy scheme of things, simply on my account. But of course it can't be. It's just a rush of oestrogen through the capillaries. Love: must be.

The Bloomsday Gallery has sold four of Walter's paintings – landscapes – to a dealer in New York, a director of the Manhatt. [sic] Centre for the Arts. They actually managed to get their prices up to £1000 each. Sixty per cent of £4000 is £2400 – give or take a bit, as Barley would say; he being quick if cavalier with figures. 'Give me the ballpark, give me the ballpark,' was his constant cry, whether buying properties for millions or a joint of meat for Sunday dinner.

The Manhatt. want to mount a one-man exhibition of his work, and Walter to go over to New York for the private view. He paints with a rare maturity for someone so young, they say. 'You have been *discovered*!' I say.
'I believe I have,' he says, wreathed in smiles.

Lady Juliet is on the wall, staring down at us. She has a sweet expression, and the necklace, with its sometimes brilliant, sometimes glowing colours, changing as the autumn sun moves across the skylight, glitters and flickers emerald-green and blue-sapphire and red-ruby in the good North light, and seems to move on her flesh. She could almost be breathing.

16

Walter Wells was indeed over the moon. Everything in his life seemed to be going right. He had met the love of his life, and she didn't mind the cold, she understood what he was talking about, entranced him physically, and let him get on with his work. She didn't chatter or talk about herself endlessly. She had a son, but he was grown up and safely in Australia, and such was his vague understanding of genetic technology he imagined that if they ever wanted a child age would not stop her: if the scientists could clone a sheep, they could do anything. She sat for her portrait. She wore the crimson velvet dress.

'It has a distressed quality,' he said. 'It's just right for you.' He seemed to think she had suffered greatly in her life. She denied it. 'Estranged parents, a brush with bankruptcy, a gay son, a faithless husband, a spell in prison, a divorce – this hardly adds up to martyrdom, Walter.' But he insisted. She must have suffered for him to save her: he had taken her life in his hands and she had blossomed and bloomed like a rosebud when the sun came out. She didn't argue with him any more than she had with Barley.

* * *

She paid his bills, and he never had to ask her to. She did not interfere, or try to tidy up or impose her way of living on his. She took their washing home to her apartment to do it there so it didn't pile up in heaps in the bathroom. It was a dreary, over-heated, enervating place, and he could use it for the overflow of all the things he loved to have but in the end there would be no space for if they were to get from the door to the bed, and he liked a clear area round his easel.

'Whenever you go out,' she remarked, 'you come back with some new treasure.' He would find bits and pieces in skips, or in junk shops, or behind gates; or sometimes total strangers would hand them to him – a broken vase, a chipped plate, a three-legged chair, a ragged rug, a pewter mug, a tallboy with a door missing; all once perfect things he liked to live with the better to save them from the world's disregard, as others took in lost cats or dogs.

They went walking on a beach, and he found washed up on empty sands an old ship's figurehead left there by last night's gale – seventeenth century, Walter reckoned – a bleached wooden lady with her nose worn away; her breasts smooth and round as Pamela Anderson's, proud to face storms.
'The universe offers you gifts,' she suggested.
'I am one of nature's scavengers,' he said. 'That's all. I'm here to sweep up gold dust. I just see what others could if only they had eyes for it.'

He introduced her to his friends. She was nervous. He so young and she so old. But word got round that she was Grace Salt, famous, the millionaire's wife, the one in the papers for trying to mow down the mistress; hadn't she gone to prison? And she must be rich. So many factors entered in, ordinary judgements hardly applied. Mostly they viewed her through a pleasant dope haze, anyway. They tended to be late-twenties, out of art school or jazz courses: they stuck together, fuzzily, in the too hard-edged consumerist world their parents had made for them. Grace was sweet, she was pretty, she smiled a lot: she made their friend www:/ happy and now he had a show of his own in New York. Little flashes of envy and spite sometimes shot across their horizons like shooting stars in a dawn sky, but not often.

17

At Bulgari the Italian lady of a certain age with the really good simple suit and the well coiffed hair looked after them. They sat in a softly lighted cubicle, and had her full attention to themselves, and were served tea and macaroons. If she wanted to show a piece of jewellery she nodded gently to an assistant, an obliging, pretty girl with good legs but not as good as Doris's, and it appeared within minutes. Certainly, it was not out of the question, though very unusual, for the firm to contact Lady Juliet and see if she wanted to relinquish ownership of the very special piece she had in her possession. They did not object to being used as an intermediary, such was their concern for their customers, and they might charge a small commission for the service – unless of course Lady Juliet wanted a piece to replace it, in which case commission would be waived. But Barley and Doris must realise that it was rather like asking a mother to give up a loved child for adoption and not likely to happen.

Lady Juliet's piece was known as 'The Egyptian', they were told: it was an important piece, seminal to the jewellery design of the early seventies. Naturalistic motifs – lotus flowers, for example – were contained within geometric forms: quite a branching out for Bulgari.

'Sounds great,' said Doris brightly, but she hadn't really been listening.

'The introduction of Egyptian style into our cultural consciousness,' observed the assistant, suddenly 'that is to say extreme stylisation combined with a strong chromatism, happened after the Tutankhamun exhibition made its impact across Europe in the early seventies. It was much the same as the effect the invasion of Egypt by Napoleon a couple of hundred years back. Nobody knew why they were doing it, everyone just did it.'

Her boss raised an eyebrow at her and she shut up and blushed. 'I just so much like the look of it,' said Doris. 'Forget the back story.' And she quite liked the look of the assistant, Jasmine, who had the pale, translucent skin and haunted eyes of the dedicated student of art history: Doris wondered if she mightn't go far as a TV researcher. As it happened, Doris was looking for a new one for the programme. Flora Upchurch, who had been working on the show for a couple of years, was going to have to go. She was getting above herself. There had been an incident at a Requisitions Meeting lately in which Flora had pointed out to Doris that she had got Rubens and Rembrandt muddled up. Flora should not have done that. And she would not find herself forgiven for having come to Barley and Doris's wedding all long legs and short white dress, and upstaged the bride; and been caught catching and keeping Barley's eye a second too long. Doris was biding her time. But soon the axe would fall. There might be some trouble with the Head of Department, because Flora was a sly puss and had wormed her way in to everyone's good books but no-one could tell Doris how to behave any more: her ratings were too high. Doris did as she pleased. Flora would go as soon as someone halfway decent turned up – this Jasmine might just be the one. She had the right kind of tough delicacy. And she would not be working for this lot if she wasn't top notch.

But Doris should be thinking about herself, not others. She was not pleased to be told now that it was not possible to make the exact copy of a piece made exclusively for another client: something similar, of course, could be contrived. Miss Dubois was quite right: there was no inevitable moral ownership invested in every element of a jewellery design, but a law-suit to prove it might cost more than the jewellery in question. Was it the stones, or the design, or the shape which so appealed, as a matter of interest?
'Miss Dubois is accustomed to having what she wants,' said Barley, mildly.

Miss Dubois asked how long it would take to make up a piece based on the Egyptian design with as few variations as Bulgari could tolerate – they were talking a good half million here by now and if you were paying that much you deserved something, surely, and Bulgari said they could bring the time down to four or five months but craftsmen could not and would not and should not be hurried. They were quite firm, while remaining impeccably polite. The older lady even nodded to the younger, who slipped away and came back with the Director: some customers would take from men the bad news they could not accept from women.

The order was placed. Doris would wait, or said she would.

On the way home she said to Barley, 'There must be some way round this,' but Barley, quite honestly, was thinking of other things.

18

Walter Wells put down his paintbrush and looked at his finished composition. He was pleased with it. Grace shone out from the canvas; she'd said he flattered her and made her look younger than she was. He'd said he painted only what he saw. He took a turpentine-soaked rag and wiped some titanium white off his fingers. He had achieved the presence and colour of his loved one's velvet dress by glazing, then daring to fleck Roman red oils with tips of pink-white acrylic, rather as if they were waves of the sea; there was movement and texture there and he felt what he thought Van Dyck must have thought when he finished the portrait of Charles I and Henrietta Maria with their two eldest children in 1632, lace ruffs, cloth of gold and all: if I can do this I can do anything.

Wiping his fingers had made matters worse, not better, for the rag was already sodden with assorted paint, from Lady Juliet's portrait right back to a seascape finished a year ago, and though it removed white, it left a smear of greeny grey behind instead. He tissued the smear off and noticed, to his pleasure, that his hands no longer seemed pale and tender like a child's – they were a man's hands, strong and decisive. Since he'd met Grace he'd grown up.

Grace was round at her service flat in Tavington Road doing their washing. He was used to going to the launderette and shoving everything in at once and putting the temperature to ninety: she liked to separate whites from blacks and do everything at forty degrees. She was like his mother. He would take her down to visit his parents soon: he had told his mother on the phone that he 'had met someone' and now he would have to follow through. But his parents, Prue and Peter, lived in the old world of cottage gardens and retired clergy: they had a little house near the Cathedral Close in Salisbury: having an artist son was excitement enough. But if he had taken up with an older lady, an ex-jailbird, a woman of notoriety, however passing, and of considerable wealth, they would doubt both her character and his motives. They would wonder, as he did not, where their grandchildren were going to come from, and they had lived the kind of life in which they had given up a great deal for the future of the world – they were good people, in fact – and he could see that now to have no stake in that future would for them be hard indeed. He lived in the *now, now, now* world. They did not. And the solution of cloning was hardly going to appeal. GM crops seemed shocking enough.

They would be pleased that he had been taken up by a New York gallery, but would not understand the implications, not just for himself but for art in general. It was a good gallery indeed, which normally specialised in art installations, unmade beds as art objects and so on: this was an unexpected reversal for them, back to paintings you could hang on a wall. The decision might be more dictated by demands of space in Manhattan than anything else – the new art tended to require a lot of floor in which to spread itself – but never mind. He might end up in the Met as the new Edward Hopper, or Balthus – or good Lord, just himself: Walter Wells.

He would like there to be a Mrs Wells – not that there was much point in marriage any more, none of his partnered friends had gone through any form of ceremony, and if Grace remarried she lost her alimony. Alimony, it seemed, was payment for domestic services rendered, in this case to the capitalist monster Barley Salt, on condition that after the contract was terminated no further employment was to be sought. Very strange.

One day when Grace was away at her flat doing their washing, what looked like a raven alighted on the skylight above him. The light was going, so probably he'd done as much as he could to her portrait – it really needed to be taken down from the easel and a blank canvas put up in its place, ready for the next inspiration, but he liked just seeing her there: it was company when she was out. He was eating a baked potato – Grace had put it in the microwave for him, so all he had to do was work out the timer: he felt the need to eat as soon as he had put down his brush – a matter of input out and input in, one art, the other food – when this dark shadow moved over him, yellow eyes gleamed at him, and there was the raven, a giant black bird, staring down at him. He was accustomed to crows – his father had even been driven to go shooting them, whilst claiming that he hated taking the life of any living thing but they'd nest in the tall trees and drive out the song birds and the sparrows – but this creature, this presumed raven of myth and legend and the Tower of London, was on an altogether different scale from a mere crow. He decided, as it flew off, that its image had been magnified by some happenstance of glass and light, and felt oddly relieved. All the same he shivered. Then he thought that since the portrait was finished – he'd used a mixture of acrylics and oils, and the white flecks were in acrylic and would have dried by now – he'd throw its protective cloth over it – a length of light natural linen cloth he was accustomed to using for this purpose.

He finished his baked potato, leaving the skin. His mother had always encouraged him to eat the skins of potatoes since that was where their Vitamin C lurked, and had the peasants not peeled them the Irish Famine would not have been so terrible a thing. The phone rang. He had finished work so he answered it. Normally he would have left it, let it ring. People soon gave up and went away if you didn't answer after one or two attempts. He did not have an answerphone, let alone a fax or e-mail. The easier communication was, he had decided, the more unnecessary the things that were communicated.

It was Doris Dubois. He recognised her voice from the TV. Hers was one of the few programmes he watched, and he quite liked her, though she bounced about rather in her enthusiasms. But at least she had them, and wasn't forever bad-mouthing everything in a supercilious way, and when on occasion she branched out from books into art what she had to say was interesting and plausible. Grace had told him – she refused to watch – that in that case Doris Dubois must have some very good researchers working for her to whom she gave no credit, but Grace, normally so kind and charitable, was not quite to be trusted when it came to Doris Dubois. She had taken off her dress and given it to auction for charity and he'd thought that was a noble gesture. She had no idea, of course, or he supposed she had not, that her husband's previous wife was now living with him. But why should she mind that? First wives can hold grievances against second wives, and there were films to prove it but, why should second wives envy the first?

'Walter Wells the painter?'

'Yes. Is that Doris Dubois?'

'You recognise my voice?'

'It's very well known.' It was always sensible to flatter a little, while playing for time.

'Well thank you, Walter. I liked your portrait of Lady Juliet. You do jewellery and fabrics so well.' She had the same instinct, it seemed. 'I'm looking for something to give my husband Barley Salt for his birthday – in December, he's Sagittarius though you wouldn't think it – and I thought you might do a portrait of me.'

'What, to give to him?' asked Walter. 'The painting is usually a present from the person in the couple who hasn't been painted.'

'I don't see why. It means at least Barley doesn't have to pay for it. Who paid for Lady Juliet's?'

'Her husband, of course.'

'How much do you charge?'

He thought of the New York gallery, he thought of Grace paying his bills, he thought how nice it would be to be free of worry, to leap to the next income bracket of portrait painters; and said, 'Twelve thousand pounds.'

There was silence at the other end. Then: 'But that's absurd. I know for a fact that you got paid £1800 for two paintings, one for real for Lady Juliet and a copy for auctioning. Your prices can't have gone up so much in three months.'

'Well, they have. Also it's a question of time. I can't just drop everything and do this for you by December.'

'Can I come round and talk to you about it?'

'No.'

'I'm coming anyway,' she said.

19

I must write to Carmichael. I will tell him what has happened. The antipodes will hear of it. South of the equator will ring to the news. I will tell him his mother is happy again and has found new love with a man. He might be more excited if her new love was a woman, but never mind. Shall I also tell him that the man is scarcely older than he is? I think not. And that Walter looks like him, that I thought he was gay, until we took the painting back to this studio and he kissed me? And we ended in bed. No. That is enough to turn any son into Hamlet.

Separate the black from the white: the black T-shirts to one side, the white socks and shirts to the other. White is not the right word for them any more, years of mixed washes have left them a desolate grey, but if they are washed separately and very hot, some of their initial brightness might return. Hot means time, though, waiting. I could answer the letters that pile up this side of the door but really I can't be bothered. That old world seems so unreal. I could pray, and thank God for my blessings. If you pray 'Dear God help me now,' on the way to prison in a mobile cell, never having given Him two thoughts before in all your life, which seems cheating, and prison does not turn out to be quite the unendurable place you thought, not quite, then perhaps you should send a word of gratitude in His direction. You might need Him again. And manners matter, as my mother would say.

A great oversized crow has just alighted on the windowsill and stared in at me with orange eyes. And then it made a kind of short sharp desperate high-pitched cry and flew off. Enough to frighten anyone. But I'd read about it in the papers. It's only some kind of overlarge jackdaw with a very long tail which has escaped from the Zoo. A special kind of magpie from the African savannah, that's all, missing home and warmth. Nothing supernatural here, it just makes one uneasy, casting so great a shadow. It's the city equivalent, the bird version, of the puma that people see in the country when they've taken too many drugs: the creature too big to be a cat that leaps through the open window and sits staring on the dressing table in the moonlight, and the minute, petrified, they get to the light switch it's gone. It's the animal loping across the lawn in the evening, might be a very big dog but it's the wrong shape. It's the feline paw prints in the mud where the sheep have been devoured in the lonely middle of the moor. Whatever it is, it's gone, thank God. Not much use reporting a sighting, birds fly where they will. It may, they say in the papers, stop haunting the borough and just fly home again to its cage. They have left the door open. There's warmth, shelter and food to be had in there. There were women in my prison who preferred it inside to out, for these three things. I wish the bird well, for all it frightened me. Few things are evil but thinking makes them so.

*   *   *

I want Carmichael's approval. I doubt that I'll get it. My friends, my erstwhile friends – it's true most drifted off when I went to prison and who can blame them? – would tell that sons hate it when their mothers remarry, and turn into Hamlets all. Worse, Walter is an artist, which I know Carmichael has always wanted to be, even though he has never done anything about it but took to sewing instead. Barley laughed at one of Carmichael's early paintings – a head with arms coming out where the ears should be, which is of course how three-year-olds do paint people – but Barley scoffed, and said, 'Can't you do better than that? That looks like an octopus.' And Carmichael took offence and never painted again. Other women's children took home child art: Carmichael never gave me that pleasure. His pleasure lay, quite frankly, in stitching up his father.

Time to take the duvet out of the dryer – stretch the arms wide, bringing corner to corner, running finger and thumb along the seam to keep it straight – patience is needed, getting the edges exactly together or all faults become magnified and the end result is a bulky mess. Laundry was sent by God as moral instruction: discuss.

I no longer go to the gym. Really there isn't time. I get more than enough exercise as it is, running up and down to the studio, over to the flat and back, round the markets looking for the cheapest oranges, lugging bags of laundry, and that's leaving sex out of it. I could be young again: all I miss is a small child tugging on my arm. I have more energy than I did. So much happiness can do for you. I even bled a little at the full moon, as if my body were in acute remembrance of things past. I would always bleed at the full moon, in sympathy with the wheeling cosmos. I would have liked more children but never conceived after Carmichael, and Barley would tell me one was enough.

I remember Barley coming home one summer evening and finding Carmichael bent over a piece of cloth, sewing button-holes. I couldn't understand at the time, knowing as he did how his father hated this kind of thing, that Carmichael, only nine, did not take himself and his work inside as soon as Barley's car appeared at the end of the drive. I supposed you couldn't expect this kind of deceit from a totally honourable nine-year-old; that he was hoping, poor child, that his father would approve, examine the button-hole and say 'How admir-able! I'm proud of you; just like your mother!' But a window broken with a cricket ball would have seemed more natural to Barley and met with more approval.

The laundry's done, the lights are off, time to go home. Mr Zeigler the porter says 'Don't see much of you anymore, Mrs Salt.'
I say, 'Oh, I'm staying round the corner with a friend.'
He looks at me for once as if he sees me, which is more than he usually does; we're all just different versions of the same tenant to him, forever wanting washing machines repaired, or noises stopped, or messages passed, and he could do his job a lot better if it wasn't for us, and he wishes me well.

20

Walter Wells went quickly to the door when he heard Grace coming up the stairs. These days she almost ran, he noticed. She would take the stairs two at a time. He'd slowed down a lot, and even got aches in the backs of his legs. His father had complained a lot of these. Perhaps it was coming to him prematurely. He wanted to forewarn Grace about what she would see when she went into the studio; he didn't want her upset. What she would see would be Doris Dubois sitting on the chair where once Grace had so recently sat to have her portrait painted, and before that Lady Juliet Random. Now on the easel, off the wall, was Juliet's portrait, her face already half blanked out by titanium white, which is a good background for most flesh tints and Doris, it had to be admitted, had a good, clear, healthy complexion, as energy and determination poured through every cell; it might not be an agreeable energy but it was certainly there.

He waylaid Grace on the third landing. The studio was on the fourth. He took the bag of clean washing from her. She would iron it in the studio. Neither of them wanted servants, strangers, in.

*   *   *

'Now Grace,' he stood there saying, looking very mature and trustworthy and not the least like Carmichael any more. How could she ever have thought he was gay? 'You have to understand this: don't scream or shout or anything, the way women do in films, but Doris Dubois is in our studio and I am painting her portrait. But not her entire portrait, only her face on Lady Juliet's body.'

'But why?'

'To save me time and her money,' said Walter. 'Mind you, she has a very busy schedule too. She came unasked to discuss prices, saw Lady Juliet upon the wall, my easel without a canvas, and demanded that I start painting her then and there.'

Grace sat down on the stairs. She felt quite calm. She felt her future stretched in front of her, full of infinite events and variations of these events.

'As Goya painted the Duke of Wellington's head over that of Napoleon's brother,' she said, 'when news came that the Duke of Wellington, the conquering hero, had arrived at the gates of the city. At least there is some precedent here.'

Walter Wells sat down beside her on the stairs. Grace breathed in the smell of oil paint, baked potato, tobacco, and even now, with its overtone of Doris Dubois's favourite Giorgio perfume, which Doris had worn in court; she loved it.

'I didn't know Goya did that,' said Walter.

'Oh yes,' she said. 'A painter has to live.'

They held hands. Hers was young and soft and helpless in his.

'You get younger every day,' he said. 'I didn't want to do it but she insisted.'

'What bribes and sanctions did she use?' asked Grace.

'If I do this for her she will give me a slot on her TV show.'

'A whole programme to yourself or a five minutes slot? The first is something, the second is nothing.'

'She didn't say. And she offered to sleep with me but of course I declined.'

'Politely, I hope,' said Grace, with considerable calm. 'Hell hath no fury and she's furious enough as it is. What were her threats?'

Grace, to her own surprise, felt encouraged rather than intimidated. She had her enemy trapped. Doris Dubois had put a foot too far and ended up unarmed in hostile territory.

'She was not specific: just that she knew the Director of Tate Modern well, and the Summer Exhibition would close its doors to me.'

'She is certainly a powerful person in the art world,' said Grace. 'I reckon we'd better go in and face her. Does she know I'm living with you?'

'I don't think so,' said Walter. 'But all things are possible. She is the *Gestalt* of our times. She will have informers everywhere.' And they went on in.

'Well, well, well,' said Doris Dubois. 'It's the murderess. You do get around. If I was superstitious I'd say you were the Hound of Hell pursuing me and have you put back in prison for a stalker.'

Doris Dubois sat on the plinth where her rivals Lady Juliet and Grace Salt had lately sat, draped in a length of blackout cloth. From the canvas on the easel Lady Juliet's Bulgari necklace gleamed out, a source of power and influence.

'I see what it is,' said Grace. 'You're not trying to save money.

From what's going on at the Manor House that is the last of your concerns. You are after Lady Juliet's necklace. You think it's magic. You think if you own it you will turn into a person everyone likes, whether you deserve it or not. You will even put up with Lady Juliet's body in order to have that.'

'I have Barley's love,' retorted Doris, 'which is more than you do any more, if you ever did. I think he was only ever sorry for you. And now you are reduced to buying a younger man, a toyboy.'

Doris Dubois was a little shaken, all the same. She had expected Grace to cringe and be frightened, and afraid that she, Doris, would run off with Walter Wells as well as her husband. But no. And had Doris not just recently been polled the nation's sweetheart, and been asked to compère the Eurovision Song Contest the following year? Everyone loved and wanted Doris, it was patently evident. Why then did Grace's words cut her to the quick?

'Good Lord,' said Grace, 'I'm sure there's less of a gap between me and Walter than there is between you and my ex-husband.'

Grace was folding laundry in the corner of the room, busy with domestic tasks, as if Doris's presence was neither here nor there, though indeed her injured heart was seething. As for Walter, he'd put on his Rembrandt hat, which kept his ears warm, and was checking through his squeezed, squashed, metallic tubes of paint. Label printing had flaked away beneath the assault of turpentine and hard moist fingers: he could only tell the colours by peering at the congealed ring of paint beneath the tubes' lopsided lids. He wished he had chosen to be a poet not a painter: life seemed suddenly altogether too difficult.

'It's normal for a man to marry someone younger than he is. It's not for a woman.'

'Then it should be,' said Grace, briskly. 'Walter, do just get on with Doris's head. The sooner it's done the sooner she'll be out of here.'

Walter took up his place at the easel. Doris let a length of very long, slim leg appear beneath the blackout cloth. Walter tried not to notice. Doris flashed him a glorious smile.

'I shall charge you for the frame, of course,' said Grace. 'That Lady Juliet painting is technically mine, though everyone seems to have forgotten about that. I paid for it.'

'You have such a mercenary nature,' said Doris Dubois. 'Driving poor Barley into the ground the way you did, screwing him for everything he had. You paid, but it was Barley's money. You live off it too, Walter, I daresay. She's bought you.'

'A pity about the body,' was all Grace said, folding away. 'Everyone will think you're a size fourteen.'

Doris, focused as she was on the necklace, had forgotten about that. 'Walter will paint along edges, won't you, and make me narrower,' she said. For every problem Doris had a solution. Her mind worked fast.

Walter murmured his assent.

'It's going to be a birthday present for Barley,' said Doris. 'Sometime in December.'

'I bet you don't know what day,' said Grace.

'Bet you do,' said Doris, nastily. 'You poor thing. If you're living your reject life in this dump with Walter I think Barley should be told. It may well affect your alimony.'

'Tell you what,' said Walter, suddenly. 'I could work just as well from a Polaroid: I'd be able to concentrate.'

'Suits me,' said Doris. 'I'm not like Grace, I don't have all the time in the world.'

*   *   *

So Walter took a Polaroid of Doris, and said the painting would be finished within the week. Grace felt quite jealous and uneasy when Walter took the photograph: it seemed too much like foreplay for comfort, as if Walter were extracting some part of Doris's essence for his own diversion, with her consent. To paint Doris Dubois could be seen as Walter's work and was therefore just about excusable – how many crimes seem justified not just by money but by sheer professionalism: *that's only business*, says the Mafia victim as he dies: *the hit man's only doing his job.* Of the public executioner on Death Row, *a real professional, born to it!* But for Walter to take a photograph, to watch Doris appearing out of nothing, first a blur, then clearly defined on a square of greasy paper, seemed too intimate by half. Grace knew she was being ridiculous but you felt what you felt.

After Doris Dubois had gone, trit-trotting on her smart heels down the studio stairs, Grace cried and cried as if she were a child, great pity-me sobs, she felt so polluted and robbed.

'You were magnificent, Grace, magnificent!' soothed Walter. Grace noticed a single white hair in his eyebrows, found her tweezers and pulled it out and soon they were happy again.

21

'Barley darling,' said Doris Dubois to her husband, 'Do you think I'm a nice person?'

Barley considered this question with care. They lay in a big bed with an elaborate headboard and pale brocade curtains in Claridges Hotel, in Brook Street, Mayfair, and waited for breakfast. Outside, London roared by. The bathroom was marble and its fixtures heavy and pale: water gushed from the taps, and there was no danger of the ceiling falling in. They could relax.

'It's not the first word I'd use to describe you,' he said. 'But what's the problem? A woman doesn't have to be nice to be loved by a man. Look at Grace, I'm sure she's the nicest woman in the world but I love you, not her.'

'I'd quite like people to like me,' she said. 'All the same.'

'Your public love you,' he said. 'Look at your ratings.'

But he knew what she meant. Barley only made enemies when he had to – otherwise he worked on the principle that you were helpful to the elevator boy on the way up because you were very likely to meet him on the way down. But it was in

Doris's nature to cut swathes through people's ordinary desire to be co-operative and do their best, however imperfect that best might be. She had made an enemy of Ross the chauffeur by giving him a diet sheet, and saying if he didn't lose weight Barley was going to have to fire him. The incompetence of Belgradia Builders, as they called themselves, was exacerbated by her reporting one of their number to the Immigration Authorities. The daily cleaner Grace and he had employed for fifteen years, Helen, had finally walked out, partly out of loyalty to Grace but mostly because Doris refused to pay her in cash, and then when Helen went to Barley for help, reporting her to Inland Revenue for tax fraud.

He'd liked Helen. She was stout and plain and stubborn which was why Doris couldn't put up with her. When he told her he was marrying Doris she'd shrugged and said, 'Don't worry about me, I don't care who lies in the bed, I just get to make it.' The teams of professional cleaners Doris now brought in to service Wild Oats sucked the soul out of the new carpets with their industrial vacuum machines, and wore the new paintwork away by the energy of their efforts, cost ten times what Helen had done, and for all he knew were as sharp of tongue as Helen but he did not understand the many languages they spoke. And why were the carpets down, in any case, while Belgradia Builders were still trampling in and out, which so far as he could see would be forever? They spent more time on their cellphones talking to Amnesty International than they did actually building anything. He would never have employed them himself, but Doris wouldn't be told.

Here all was peace and quiet. Claridges seemed better able to control its workforce than Doris did hers, as even she was beginning to admit. As Barley had predicted, there was now trouble with the Insurance Company, to the tune of some £250,000, funds better spent getting back on his feet should the Opera Complex scheme collapse. In the small print of the policy was a clause requiring that major renovation be undertaken only by approved builders recognised by the Guild of Master Builders, and of course the firm chosen by Doris – on the grounds that they'd presented the lowest tender had never so much as heard of this body.

Doris's assertion that what was being done to Wild Oats could in no way be described as 'major' – 'major' surely meant stripping a house to its foundations, which everyone should know Doris had in her time done – met with raised eyebrows and stony faces. Not even Barley's cheery greetings and bonhomie could move them, in their august and impassive buildings in Holborn.

'You know how it's the Insurance Companies are funding so much of this anti-social, élitist research into longevity,' said Doris to her friend the Producer at work. 'How about a hard-hitting documentary on the subject? We could get the law changed.' But even this did not serve to make them change their mind. Barley Salt might be a power in the land of development, and in his time had been to tea both at the Palace and Downing Street, and Doris Dubois might be an opinion-former *par excellence*, but Insurance kept its own counsel and had its own rules, which applied to influential and celebrity clients just as it did to anyone else.

But here in Claridges these bothers could be forgotten. There were white fluffy towels in abundance, traditional water-colours on the wall, complimentary champagne, exotic fruit in the glass bowl with a gold-embossed card from the management bidding them welcome. After a night's wild sex and the happy sleep that follows it, they now lay back naked side by side against plump down pillows, lace-trimmed, he so male and broad and hairy, she so soft and narrow and pliant, and talked about this and that. Really, thought Doris, it's okay here. I could live the simple life.

They would not go back to Wild Oats until Belgradia Builders were finished, she told Barley: in the meantime Doris would leave everything to the architect she had now brought in to supervise them, or rather his Project Manager, who would just have to get on without her help.

But after this exchange, after the waitress had removed the orange juice and fat-free yoghurt and decaff on which they had breakfasted in bed, after the flow of maids and minibar attendants had died away, after the *Do Not Disturb* notice had been put on the door handle and they could turn their attention to making love again, delight failed them. For some reason Barley's body failed to respond to his mind's inclinations: no matter how Doris coaxed and teased his languid member, it remained uninterested: Doris, a fever of expectation herself, remained unsatisfied, indeed, actually un-entered. Their day had to begin, for once, without the intoxication of sex.

She did not show her disappointment to Barley. She knew there were troubles looming in his business life, to do with Lady Juliet, Lord Random and Billyboy Justice, and that they were worse than he'd imagined. She'd had a rather worrying conversation in the Green Room after the show with the new Minister for Culture – whose department's ever-changing department brief now included Sports, Scientific Research and

Waste Disposal – to the effect that the Lottery was pulling out of Arts and putting its funds into New Science and technology. She'd said nothing to Barley. Sexual malfunction was often to do with 'business worries'. It would probably be all right in the end. But he was rather older than her; and it was beginning to show.

Barley showered and dressed, and Ross the chauffeur called up from the Lobby. Barley had a meeting at eleven with the building contractors in relation to the Opera Noughtie project. There was a certain amount of Russian money – which these days meant Mafia money – already invested. He suspected it was because they had translated 'Noughtie' as 'Naughty' and believed they were into some kind of new State Brothel project: as it was, it was meant to be a celebration of the first ten years of the *New Millennial Century in the Arts*. The joke gave him no cause to be amused. Things were tricky enough with the Russians anyway: if the project fell through there would be real trouble and Ross would have to brush up his security driving and even get a licence for a Kalashnikov or something similar, at least when they travelled abroad.

22

Walter and Grace lay wrapped in each other's arms in bed in the studio. The cotton sheets were clean and crisply ironed. They had been on the 'extra dry' cycle but, as Walter pointed out: 'You watered them with your tears.' Doris's portrait was covered with a cloth so her face could not be seen to be watching them. Walter had made her really ugly as he painted, to make Grace laugh.

'She'll be all right on the day,' he'd said. 'We can't afford to upset the client no matter how much we want to.'

'You don't need the money,' Grace had argued. 'Everything I have is yours. Just call her and say you've changed your mind.' But he had said he couldn't live off Grace, his pride would not allow it, he had to get his career going, £5000 was not to be sneezed at. And so on. Besides, the problem intrigued him. Put Doris's head on Lady Juliet's body? What sort of chimera would you produce: would a simple narrowing of the body create the illusion of slimness, or a grotesquerie? The oddness of it was strangely erotic but he didn't mention that to Grace.

*   *   *

The doorbell rang. Grace stiffened at once.

'Stay there,' said Walter, pulling on his kimono and going to the door. 'Whoever it is I'll send them away.' But when he opened the door it was to his mother and father. It was not possible to send them away, and besides, he was pleased to see them. His mother was wearing her best coat, and the uncomfortably shiny shoes she wore to town. Peter wore a jacket that he'd bought in the Seventies, and was still perfectly good; though it had seemed muted at the time, it now seemed was quite bright. But his friendly, short-sighted eyes and beakish nose were traditional enough, and his hair was sparse, as befitted a man of nearly seventy. Walter had come along late in the marriage.

'Why Walter,' said his mother. 'Is that you? Yes, of course it is. Are you all right?'

'Why shouldn't I be?' asked Walter.

'You look so old. Peter, doesn't Walter look old all of a sudden? Well, not exactly old, just not a little boy any more. Mature. Very handsome.'

'Hair's beginning to recede,' said Peter. 'Takes after me, poor fellow – more's the pity!'

In the bed, Grace pulled the sheet up to her chin. Her clothes were in the bathroom but there was no way she could get there without being seen: and she needed to clean her teeth, but you could not get to the washbasin, because the rescued ship's figurehead was in the way, so you had to use the bath.

'Mother, father –' Walter began.

'Sorry to turn up so early,' said Peter, 'But your mother insisted on coming up by coach to save money, and they don't keep social hours.'

*   *   *

Prue had gone to the easel and was looking at the portrait, with its deformed if so far sketchy version of Doris's head where Juliet's should be.

'How very peculiar,' she said. 'Is this the kind of thing you're selling to New York? I bet that piece of jewellery costs a lot. I must say it is quite well done, Walter, that bit at any rate. I always thought you had more talent for words than pictures, but Dorothy – you remember the friend I met in hospital when I was having you – rang me last night and said she'd read a snippet in the *Mail* about you being the rage in America. The oddest people read the *Mail*.'

Grace took courage and said 'Hi,' from the bed and Prue and Peter turned to look at her. 'I'm sorry,' she said, 'Look the other way. My clothes are in the bathroom. I'm Walter's girlfriend, Grace.' And she got out of bed and walked to the bathroom.

'What a nice figure,' said Prue. And it was true, Grace's figure had improved no end lately. She was positively skinny around the midriff: Walter was beginning to feed her little scraps of honeycake and almond in an attempt to fatten her up. 'Dorothy did say apparently you had a new girlfriend, rather older than yourself, too, and a not very nice piece in the *Mail* about it, but they got everything wrong, the way the papers do. That's just a slip of a girl.'

'We're not prudes or anything,' said Peter. 'We know how everything's changed, we see it on TV, it's just a new world, isn't it, but is she actually living here, or just staying overnight?'

'Living here,' said Walter. Grace came out of the bathroom, pretty and positive in T-shirt and short skirt. All said how pleased they were to meet one another. The doorbell rang, and Grace went to open it: it was her friend Ethel from prison, wearing a combat jacket and with a cardboard prison issue suitcase in her hand.

'I've nowhere else to go,' said Ethel. 'They turned me out with twelve quid and I gave it to a homeless person on the way here. He needed his drugs badly, from the look of him. I went to the address you gave me before you got out but the porter sent me on here. You're looking good. Had a face-lift or something?'

The phone rang but no-one liked to answer it.

23

Once Barley had left with Ross, Doris spent an hour on the phone. She got through to the show and asked them to contact the young art historian called Jasmine – they could find her working at Bulgari – and see if she wanted a change of job.

She called her architect and told him to take over the builders. The architect said sorry, he was pulling out of the job – he was used to difficult clients but Doris took the biscuit. Doris said she'd rather he didn't do that: not only were there VAT irregularities in his invoices which looked like wilful evasion to her: she had been paying the builders cash on his advice, and under the new Asylum Laws this was an offence punishable by prison. The architect eventually agreed that it was to be business as usual, except that he would visit the site daily, not once a week, and not leave it to his project manager. That was quite a long phone call.

She called Walter Wells but he didn't answer. That would have to stop.

*   *   *

She called Lady Juliet to see if she would sell her the Egyptian Piece but got the bum's rush. That was quite a short call.

Reckoning that Ross would have dropped off Barley by now, she called him on his cellphone and asked him the date of Barley's birthday, which she once knew but had forgotten. December twelfth. Six weeks from now. Sagittarius. She hoped Ross was sticking to the diet sheet. She hoped she didn't hear him munching. There would be a weigh-in when he called for his wages on Friday. Ross said it was time he was given a proper pension and health-care plan, if she was that worried about his welfare.
'It's way too late for all that, Ross,' said Doris.

She went down Bond Street and called in at an antique shop she knew and bought a large and very involved reddish-black mahogany fireplace in the Scottish baronial style, to be delivered to Wild Oats the next day.

She went back to Claridges and called the management because the maid was still in there hoovering, and complained about the standard of her work. She'd found a cherry pip stuck to the bottom of the bin and it was disgusting.

She was not in a good mood, and even she noticed it. But that was what sexual deprivation always did to her.

She called the designer and told him to liaise with the architect from now on. She was a public figure and owed that public her full attention. Wild Oats was to be finished by December twelfth. She was giving a surprise birthday party for Barley and everyone who was anyone would be there. The library was to be re-vamped to fit in with a big fireplace that would be delivered the next day, and pride of place given to a painting six foot by three and a half, to be delivered by December eleventh. The painting was her gift to Barley and would be unveiled during the course of the party. She did not want to hear about his problems, she just wanted the thing done.

She called Walter Wells again; the phone was answered this time, but not by him.

'Why Grace,' said Doris, 'fancy you! Tell your toyboy I need another sitting. I don't think any proper artist can work from a Polaroid. He should come round to my place in Notting Hill at five this afternoon.'

Barley should not have acted so *old*, and left her feeling so peculiar. Young men are not so easily affected by 'business worries'. Barley deserved what he got, for his discourtesy to the nation's sweetheart.

She heard a ministerial broadcast on the radio announcing cuts in the arts budget and a concomitant increase in grants to scientific research. She called Bulgari and told them to get on with it: she would be in to choose stones at one-twenty. So, everyone would just have to forgo lunch: this was England not Italy. Personally she never ate lunch.

She would have called girlfriends but she didn't have any.

24

When I was in my early thirties and Carmichael was a little boy, and Barley was in and out of bankruptcy, and sometimes we would have to pack up and go just to be ahead of our creditors, I thought that by the time I was in my fifties life would have settled down. There would be no more anguish: no more jealousies, no more going through Barley's pockets to find out where he'd been the night before. *Never ask questions if one doesn't want to know the answer.* So my mother once told me. No finding out that Barley had set up with some stupid floozie in a flat in St John's Wood: that kind of thing. And being appalled by his taste – I went to see her and what a whingey little whiner she was. Barley likes his women either placid – or so I always presented myself – or boldly energetic and awful like Doris who never lets a blade of grass grow if she can grind it underfoot.

In my head I'd been waiting around for the absurdities to stop. One day Barley would grow up, and decide to play safe; and not dangerous, both financially and emotionally. He would start worrying about his virility, and not risk the indignity of failing with a new woman, and come home to me.

I was wrong: here am I in my mid-fifties, and the roller coaster gets worse: it starts as a minor tremor, the harmonics begin to twang, join one another in surging rhythm, compounding the wave of resonance, and before you know it you're in a Bridge Over Tacoma Narrows situation, and the bridge is about to shake itself to pieces.

One day I'm spending a quiet evening at home, the next Barley comes home early and says he's in love with Doris Dubois.

My first instinct was to laugh, which of course was quite wrong.

'What's so funny about that,' he demanded.

'Darling,' I said, with a confidence I should not have had. 'She could have anyone. I don't think you're going to have much luck.'

'And she's in love with me,' he said. 'You always underrate me. You don't take me seriously. I have to go outside the marriage to find someone who does.'

And he said he wanted a divorce, and I could have the Manor House. And he was moving out, and we could all be perfectly civilised, couldn't we?

It was only after I lay in wait for Doris in the car park outside her place of work, and tried to murder her, that she decided to move in to the Manor House and change its name. My divorce proceeded more or less without me, since I was in prison; and though my lawyer came once or twice to visit me there he was quite traumatised by the noise and bedlam and crying children and the prohibited but nonetheless achieved sexual encounters of visiting hour, and the genuine tears and shame, and the passionate kissing during which drugs are passed from mouth to mouth. It was hard for him to concentrate; he was

115

accustomed to the Inns of Court and, as he kept telling me, he was a specialist in divorce, not criminal law. And I, to tell you the truth, was fairly traumatised as well, and didn't fight as hard as I should, and Doris got her way. She does get her way. Sometimes I almost admire her for it. But you have to resist that kind of thinking, as Dr Jamie Doom says. It's victim-speak: the person tortured comes to admire the skill of the torturer: almost to fall in love.

I have stopped going to Dr Doom. He says I am not 'ready', but he seems pleased for my happiness, my new roller coaster of fear and desire, and says he won't report me to the Probation Service.

I'd started by rather loathing the Manor House, when we first moved in. Barley didn't consult me before he bought it. It seemed so pretentious, so large, a challenge to the Official Receiver – but I grew to love it for its redbrick ungainliness. I knew every creepy-crawly corner of it, and had shoved my dustpan and brush along every dusty front and back stair. I knew its temperament and its habits, and that the attic stairs were haunted, and you could hear a drumming noise that shouldn't be there on Friday nights, and if you went up to find out why you'd feel a nasty chill and hear voices of people who weren't there, sometimes weeping, sometimes laughing. Other days of the week it would be okay. It never bothered me, but Carmichael would wake when he was little, and complain of a woman in white standing at the end of the bed.

And now Doris Dubois has my home and my husband to do what she wants to with them, and sleeps in the room which Barley and I once called our own. But I hear from Ross – I met him in the McDonald's next to the Health Club –

that the ceiling fell down on them and they've had to flee to Claridges. She'll like that: it's nearer the shops. Ross is trying to lose weight. Doris makes him stand on scales every Friday while he collects his pay. I give him diuretic tablets – they sometimes help.

I had thought that by the time I was in my fifties I would not be suddenly confronted by shocked older people while naked in a doubtful bed, that I would always be able to get to a washbasin to clean my teeth, that jailbird friends would not turn up to call in favours. I was wrong. In youth the convulsions of fate, fortune and love come at short intervals: as one grows older the stretches of non-event are longer, but the convulsions are more extreme, and come as tidal waves in a calm sea, rather than as little peaks of fluff and foam in choppy water. That is all that happens. Nothing changes.

What I am trying not to think about is that Doris has summoned Walter to her apartment in Notting Hill and he has gone, sketchpad under his arm, laughing at my fears. It is a worse roller coaster than any I can remember with Barley, my heart is now in my mouth, now in my boots, now banging away in my chest, I am sick to my stomach. I am an old woman, she is a young one. How can I compete? This bridge, this gleaming arrow of desire, like the one that runs between Tate Modern and St Paul's, joining the present to the past, is in danger of setting up such a resonance of harmonics it will twist and torment itself to death.

25

Grace McNab, once Grace Salt, perhaps one day to be Grace Wells – see how down and down in the alphabet she has gone in her life – was sitting in the Harley Street waiting room of Dr Chandri the cosmetic surgeon when Lady Juliet Random came in. Grace had the five o'clock appointment, Lady Juliet the five thirty.

The waiting room was very dull: a big round table in the middle, with neat unread piles of *Country Life* and some stiff upright chairs pulled up to it. There was plumbing that showed. On the walls were before-and-after photographs of women – once with odd noses, and chins, and saggy eyes and fat-humpy backs, but now all looking at least ordinary, if not startlingly beautiful. The place smelt of old-fashioned chloroform and ether. Chandri was running late. It was already five twenty-five, according to the ornate ebony clock with its carved wounded stags and baying dogs which stood on the marble fireplace. If Walter Wells had been on time he would already have been with Doris Dubois for twenty-five minutes.

* * *

Harry Bountiful would let Grace know whether or not he had been on time, and the nature of what was said at the meeting. Grace felt ashamed of having been in touch with the private detective again, but jealousy drove her to it, just as jealousy had driven her to try to mow Doris down. Nothing was made better, but if you were a person ravaged by self-doubt, it was less painful to know than to guess. What you imagined was usually worse than what happened. In someone like Doris, whose self-esteem was sky high, it would be the other way round. Unpalatable truths would come as a surprise, not as a confirmation of worst fears. Harry Bountiful had not got round to taking the bugs out of Doris's apartment, although Grace had stopped his retainer when Doris and Barley got married. What was the point? Barley would not come back. If Barley had found out she had eavesdropped on his life, he would have laughed. She did not want Walter to find out. He would not take it well.

'My dear Grace,' said Lady Juliet, 'how wonderful to see you. What are you having done? I want my nose looked at. It's much too large, as I realise whenever I look at that wonderful portrait your young Walter painted. How is all that going? You look completely glorious. Personally I think it's the sex that does it, especially all that oral sex at the beginning. Nothing like it for the complexion.'

'Walter is painting Doris Dubois' portrait,' said Grace, bleakly. 'She made him.'

'Doris does rather make people do things,' Lady Juliet agreed. 'I'm sure Barley never really wanted to leave you: it was just unlucky that of all people he should run into her. Like treading on a scorpion in one's shoe: no-one's fault, but there you are, stung and screaming. Only this morning she had the nerve to call me up and try to buy my Bulgari necklace from me, the one Ronald gave me when our son was born. As if the whole thing was about money. And no doubt poor Barley's expected to pay. I explained it was the best part of a million, it wasn't one of their everyday ready-made pieces at a tenth of the price, and even that didn't put her off. I gave her short shrift, you'll be glad to hear. Poor Barley, I have the feeling he may be in for a bit of trouble soon; he really shouldn't be spending the way she makes him. The Manor House was always a fairly beastly place but I believe it's a real nightmare now. All you can do with those old places is fill them with chintz, put in a new kitchen, stick to a couple of rooms and put up with being cosy not smart.'

'What sort of trouble?' asked Grace. 'Not the Opera Noughtie? Poor Barley!' She was on his side and anxious for him: it was quite automatic.

'Just a whisper in the wind,' said Lady Juliet. 'But I should sell that flat of yours while the alimony's up and running and put the money where Barley can't get at it. I love him dearly but you know what he's like.'

'Yes, I do,' said Grace, and then Dr Chandri appeared, all charisma and glow and soft eyes, and it was her turn to go in the consulting room. Lady Juliet beamed and said she had all the time in the world to spare, no-one was to hurry on her account, and opened a *Country Life* to show she meant it.

Chandri – he liked his patients to call him simply Chandri – was a sculptor as well as a surgeon. Stone artworks of lovely ladies, as he described them in his brochure, stood here and there about the consulting room, with their gallery labels still on them – Tokyo, Ontario, New York, Berlin – women rendered into massive, shiny granite. But he liked to work with the living body best of all. To join with another in the search

120

for beauty was a wonderful thing. God had given him the gift of loveliness – and he was indeed good-looking, in a plumply soulful, olive skinned, Hare Krishna, mesmerising kind of way – and also the longing to share it. He had Grace's file open in front of him.

'Do I have this wrong? Mrs Salt's daughter, perhaps?'

'I am Mrs Salt, though now I am known as Grace McNab.'

He had pictures of her, full face and profile, taken when she had been to see him last. 'So you didn't trust me! You chose another surgeon. He did a good job, whoever he was.' He was generous. He could afford to be.

'I didn't see anyone else,' said Grace, 'I just decided not to go ahead.'

'There is no letter to that effect in the file. You broke the appointment.'

'I'm sorry,' said Grace. She had forgotten that. 'I was in rather a state at the time.'

So she had been. It was in the month after Barley had told her he was going. Helen the cleaner, discovering her weeping in the bed, had told her she wasn't surprised, that she'd let herself go, told her to go on a diet and have her face done, her eyes opened, her chin lifted, buy some decent clothes, and fight back. While her sister Emily – still just about talking to her at the time, but that was before the trial and the sentence – had told her not to trivialise herself, and how well rid she was of Barley. Helen had won, Grace had consulted Chandri, and then other eventualities had come to pass. In prison you could just about get out to have your teeth fixed if you had toothache, forget cosmetic surgery.

'It's hard to believe this person in front of me and the person in the photographs is the same person,' said Chandri. 'Your eyes are twice the size, the skin is taut of its own accord, the neck is smooth.'

He seemed put out. He felt behind her ears for scars and there were none. His voice rose to a high pitch. The olive skin became quite red and dark as blood suffused it. He accused Grace of being a journalist trying to catch him out, of being a terrorist feminist, an anti cosmetic surgery hysteric. They had paid her to come along, posing as her mother, to see if he noticed. He looked round for hidden cameras and tape recorders. He demanded to see in her bag. Grace opened it, obligingly. There was nothing electronic in it, only tissues and lipsticks and post-its and keys and pens, credit cards and old receipts, as in any innocent person's bag.

'Other people recognise me,' she said, reasonably. 'Lady Juliet Random knows me well. She's outside in the waiting room. Shall we ask her in?'

But Chandri would have none of that. He did not want Lady Juliet, an excellent client, exposed to this unpleasantness.

'I was unhappy at the time, and I am happy now,' said Grace, firmly. 'That's all it is.' And as she said it, she knew it to be true. The misery of the past was trying to seep through into the present and destroy it. She was being obsessive and unreasonable: Walter could very well paint Doris Dubois and not be seduced by her, not even like her one bit. Harry Bountiful would have nothing to report: she should not have sent him in, she should not have doubted Walter: she should trust to love and leave it at that. Grace wanted to find Walter and tell him she was sorry. She wanted to leave this madman's consulting room at once: only good manners prevented her from rising there and then. The fewer manners the surgeon had, the more she would have. She was cross with herself: she had sought out Chandri in panic and desperation, hoping for a transformation, longing for youth, believing this was the way to keep Walter. But she was in no danger of losing Walter anyway. Even thinking that a face-lift would draw Barley back to her had made more sense. Barley put a premium on youth: Walter did not.

'I am in love,' she said soothingly. 'That changes people.' The statement seemed to calm the surgeon. His face returned to its proper colour: his voice fell to its normal level of serenity, calculated to inspire trust.

'Love,' he said. 'Ah, love.'

He took her into his surgery, a small white room full of mysterious electronic equipment and there, with the help of his pretty nurse, scanned and measured and photographed her face from this angle and that. He fed details into a computer. He printed out a computer image. He seemed pleased with himself.

'This process is usually done in reverse,' he said. 'But I am such a master of technology the computer holds no terrors for me. I have taken your current face and aged it by twenty years,' he said, 'and it turns into the photographs of you I have on file, taken two years ago. See for yourself.'

Grace obligingly studied the photographs. There seemed very little difference to her between one set of images and the other. You grew so familiar with your own face in the mirror, it was hard to distinguish between what you saw today and what you'd seen in the past, what was recollection and what was happening now.

'You mean I'm growing younger not older?' she asked.

'That would be a miracle,' said Chandri, and his voice faltered, but he went on bravely. 'And here in the West miracles do not happen.' He was hurrying her out of the door. 'Let me just say you do not need my services. I am known to be a man of integrity and cannot take money on false pretences. Should you change your mind and let me know the name of the surgeon who operated, I would not charge you for this appointment. To do all this and leave no scar – there was no talk of gene therapy?'

'None,' said Grace. What was the point of argument? Chandri did well enough by Lady Juliet but she would not trust her own face to him, and was glad she had not done so in the past. The man was an hysteric.

Grace dismissed the episode from her mind and hurried home to see if Walter was back, but he was not.

26

Ross met Harry Bountiful at the Juice Bar of the Health Club. Grace had recommended the place, and its excellent swimming pool, to both men. They sat on adjoining stools and fell into conversation over red grape juice, last orders before the place closed. The stools were high, hard and narrow, and Ross's backside flowed uncomfortably around his, but Harry managed well enough. He had the leanness of Humphrey Bogart, and quite looked like him too. Of all available juices, both agreed, red grape was the most like wine, and gave the illusion of some kind of nourishment. Ross explained he was on a diet imposed by his boss's new wife. Harry said sod that for a laugh he wouldn't put up with it, he'd hand in his notice; Ross said he was sorely tempted but felt too sorry for his boss to leave him.

Harry said he was trying to give up smoking because in his kind of work it was important to be able to leave a room quickly and cleanly and not leave a lingering smell of tobacco in the air. A client had told him that swimming helped kick the habit. Both men complained about the smell of chlorine which pervaded the bar, and which no amount of joss sticks could disguise, and went off to have a proper drink and a bar snack. After a couple of beers each, Harry bought a pack of cigarettes and Ross ordered a bar snack of fish, chips and peas.

It was a gay pub, and noisy, so the two heterosexual men skulked in a dark corner, tried not to draw attention to themselves, and leaned together so they could hear one another speak.

Ross let it be known that his boss's new wife was Doris Dubois and Harry nearly fell off his chair. He said he'd spent that very evening listening to Doris Dubois in conversation and otherwise with an artist called Walter Wells. He had the tape in his pocket.

'Walter Wells!' said Ross. 'But that's the young guy Grace Salt moved in with.'

'That's right,' said Harry. 'She's my client.' And they marvelled at the coincidence that had brought them together, which of course was no coincidence at all.

'Well that puts me in a quandary,' said Ross. 'Do I tell Barley Salt that his new wife's having it off with this Walter Wells or not?'

He scraped up the last of his peas, rolling them first in the remnants of his tartare sauce; there was an agreeable greeny-golden swirl at the bottom of his plate: food is such a richness of delights. It is hard to give up.

'I don't know yet what went on,' said Harry. 'Because I haven't listened to the tape. Grace didn't want me to.' She'd told him to leave it with the porter at the Tavington Road flats. He felt for it in his pocket. Yes, still there, safe. 'But since Doris asked him round to her Shepherd's Bush apartment, and they were snuck up in there alone, I guess something did. Grace certainly thinks so or she wouldn't have sent me round.'

'Doris was meant to be selling that flat,' said Ross. 'Poor old bugger Barley believes she is, anyway. Here I am, balanced on the horns of a dilemma which doesn't come easily to a man of my comfortable build. Tell? Or not to tell? He gives me the push, as bearer of bad news. Or she does, for not just not losing weight, but putting it on.'

'That's what happens,' said Harry, 'when you make a man do what he doesn't want to do. My wife left me because I wouldn't give up smoking. Told me I was giving the kids asthma. It was her being over-clean about the house which gave them asthma. Kids can do with a peck of dirt and a whiff of the old nicotine to sharpen up their lungs. The worry of it all turned me from a two pack a day guy to a four. Now I have to give up because of the job.' He coughed into his beer. Both men were in their fifties. It is hard to adapt to the new age, for some. They did try, down the health club, swimming and drinking, but the hedonism of the world as it used to be kept calling them back with its siren song.

'Tell you what,' said Ross, 'let's have a listen to that tape.'

They went back to Harry's place and listened. Since Harry's wife had left six months back he had not vacuumed a floor or washed dishes in any determined way. He kept budgerigars in a cage in the living room, which added to the musty smell. But it was cosy and womb like; they settled down with their cans of beer and crisps.

27

The tape was activated at 4.25 p.m. Microphones picked up noises around Doris's flat: the sound of a kettle, the sound of Doris undressing and showering, then the sound of a cat meowing; Doris's voice, accompanied by scuffling and what seemed to be a naked chase round the room; the noise of the shower coming and going.

'You beastly thing, how did you get in. You don't live here any more. Get out!'

The sound of china breaking.

'Now see what you've made me do! Oh, poor pussy, did I hurt you? Yuk, is that blood? I didn't know cats bled. No, you're just making a stupid fuss. There's nothing wrong with your paw or you wouldn't be purring. You belong next door. You're nothing to do with me any more. I paid her to take you in. I should have taken you to the vet and got you put down. You've no business barging in here and making me feel bad. I'm not a cat person, I told you from the beginning. Now get out, get out, get out before I take you to the vet!'

A whimper as the cat goes out the door, then a few tears from Doris.

'What could I do? Barley hates cats. I hate Barley.' The shower finally gets turned off: Country and Western on the radio. Doris sings along to *D.I.V.O.R.C.E.*.
The phone rings. The music goes off.
'Oh it's you, Flora. What do you want? Why are you calling me here? Can't you keep it to office hours? . . . No, it's not a mistake. The show doesn't need you any more. Yes, three months in lieu of notice. It's perfectly standard. Who wants disgruntled employees hanging round a TV show –? You are only on a temporary contract: all my researchers are . . . no, signing these bits of paper, or in your case not signing these bits of paper, isn't a formality, it's dire reality, darling . . . Let's just say, kindly – you're not cut out to be a TV researcher . . . I have nothing more to say on the subject. Yes, of course it's been through the proper channels. Yes, of course Alain knows: he's Head of Department. He notified Personnel. Just go away. Flora . . . I do not believe these tears.'

The phone slams down. On goes the music again; *we are family . . . all my sisters and me*: Doris dances about a bit in triumph. 'Bitch, bitch, bitch! I showed her off!' The phone goes again.
'I am not talking about this any more, Flora. This is harassment . . . Oh, it's you, Alain. Yes, I sent the papers through . . . Yes, I signed your name: we had this conversation, you remember . . . We agreed Flora had to go? Well, we did. It was an afternoon meeting. After lunch. You'd been celebrating. England had actually got a goal . . . No, I don't want her transferred. She's such a gloomy-guts: she'll spread alarm and despondency and tell tales. I want her out of the building . . . What do you mean, her legs are too good for her own good . . . ? Oh, I see, just joking. I'll tell you something about me, Alain, I don't have a sense of humour.'

The phone goes down.

'Oh Jesus, it's nearly half past. I'm not even dressed.'

The doorbell goes.

'That's okay then, that's fate ... Walter, come in. Sorry about the no clothes, it's like an oven in here. I'm not in this apartment all that much. Rather the same with Grace, I imagine, not very much in hers. Here, let me hang up your coat. You do smell nice, Walter. So male. Bet Grace likes the way you smell.'

The sound of clothes being moved around.

Walter's voice: 'You asked me here. Here I am. I can work perfectly well from the Polaroid. What do you want?'

'My hair's different. I want it the way it is now for the portrait. You have to take another Polaroid.'

'The way it is now is wet.'

The sound of a hair dryer. Doris's voice:

'Not in a minute it won't be. It was all stiff and hairdressy before. Now it's going to be free and easy, like me. My true spirit. Not all Barleyfied. God, marriage does terrible things to a girl. Don't you get tied down with Grace, she's so dull, she drove Barley to tears. What do you see in her? No, don't tell me. Money, advancement. Well, we're all a bit like that. It's a hard world, we have to survive.'

Silence. Then:

'Hold the dryer, Walter, will you, a moment, while I get my hair up ... Beneath my breasts, point it there, they're still damp from the shower ... *that feels good*, as they say in the porn films.'

The dryer is switched to full power, then turned to low power, then off. Walter's voice.

'Doris, I will take a Polaroid of your new hairstyle and then I'm going home. Nothing else.'

'You're so old and stuffy. Funny, you seemed a boy before, now you're a man. I reckon you could be as big as Picasso.

You've got such a mastery. Did I tell you, I think we're going to be able to cover your opening in New York? That's a really big deal, Walter.'

'I'm aware of that.'

'If all goes well, of course. I need the portrait for the twelfth December. Barley's birthday. I want you to be there. I'll have the media there for the unveiling. Can you do that? Of course you can. Lots of time. And remember I want the background really creeping in at the sides, to get the size eight, without any loss of artistic integrity. That'll be a turn-up for Lady Juliet. Her Bulgari on my bosom. That'll learn her not to mess with me. Then we'll fly the portrait over to New York for the opening on the sixteenth. I've fixed it with the gallery people. Can you dry my back, please?'

'It's perfectly dry already, Doris.'

'I love it when you call me Doris. So sexy and cross. All very *Déjeuner-sur-l'Herbe*, this, don't you think? Me so unclothed, you so clothed.'

'Stand still, stop dancing about, Doris, let me take this Polaroid. Your hair is exactly the same as it was before, as it happens. Then I'm going home to Grace.'

'Stay and have a drink. Straight from the can. Fizzy Orange? I haven't put any Rohypnol in it, I promise.'

She went to the fridge and opened it and in so doing disturbed one of the magnets in which one of the bugs was concealed. After that, sound was so distorted it was hard to make out what was going on.

Ross and Harry had listened in silence. Then:

'Did they or didn't they?' asked Ross.

'Hard to say,' said Harry. 'But he put up a good fight.'

'I reckon she used the Rohypnol stunt on Barley,' said Ross.

'Perhaps she tampers with the cans. That's what got the poor

131

geezer going, the night she first asked him back to her place. I drove them back, after the show. He didn't come out of there for a good six hours. I thought he was drunk, but perhaps he was drugged. He did say something about being thirsty; I remember stopping at a garage for fizzy orange on the way. Perhaps you get a taste for it.'

'But I thought with Rohypnol you were meant to forget everything. You want sex at the time, you stop being choosy, you go at it like an animal. Then you forget all about it. Sounds okay to me.'

'Your body would remember what it liked,' said Ross, 'even though your brain didn't. The next day he asked me who he'd been with the night before and I said with Doris Dubois, so he called her up and afterwards they didn't look back, and goodbye marriage, goodbye Grace. It's all my fault. I should have kept shtumm.'

They considered the matter of how the body could remember though the mind didn't, and Harry admired Ross for a romantic. Ross suggested that Harry get the canary a soul mate, it must be lonely on its own. Harry said he'd do it the next morning.

They had some more beer. Ross told Harry of his five years in the army, three as a mercenary, eight in store security, and his eventual training in bodyguard driving. Harry said if Ross ever decided to give up his job with Barley they could go into partnership. He was a loss to the world of the private investigation.

Harry and Ross took the tape round to old Mr Zeigler, the porter at Tavington Court, as arranged. They stopped on the way to have a spaghetti, and missed Ethel, returning with a tall gentleman from the Middle East wearing a camel coat and many gold rings, by minutes. She had moved into Grace's apartment, since that was the obvious place for her to stay while she found a job and somewhere to live; but she had to go out that night to earn her living the best way she could. As a girl does.

28

I hate Doris Dubois, which is reasonable, and Doris Dubois hates me, which is perverse. She wants to spoil my life. She wants what I have. She wants Barley and now she wants Walter. Just for the fun of it, to prove she can have him. Then she tosses him back to me, like a gnawed chop with a scrap of meat left on it. Why does she do it? I only met her once before she ran off with Barley. He'd given money to some arts project for disadvantaged children, and he'd taken me to the opening, and she was compèring – they paid her £5000, I later learned – and she talked to me a bit, she was being gracious. She asked me about myself and I said I didn't *do* anything, I just *was*, a housewife, waiting for her husband to come home, and yes I had a child, and house, and I liked doing the garden, and one way and another I was thoroughly boring, but I was *happy*. She said: 'You remind me of my mother,' and stalked off in a huff which surprised me. She went straight over to Barley and asked him onto her show the following month, to talk about Why Businessmen Sponsored the arts, or some such excuse.

* * *

134

He was doubtful about being on film at first, and so was I. You can be made to look such a fool on those programmes. You speak honestly and truthfully to the camera but then they put you in a context you hadn't anticipated. If Doris Dubois happened to be against private sponsorship of the arts and favoured state-subsidy, then the private sponsor – Barley, that is – could end up looking like a meddling, pretentious fool. At first Barley said no, but then Doris sent along a really pleasant researcher, an art historian, Flora by name, a pale pretty girl with very thin wrists, and we struck up quite a friendship with her, Barley and I, as sometimes couples do with single women.

Flora was interested in our Friday hauntings, and had a theory that ghosts could come out of the future, too, and were not just shadows shining through from the past. She and Barley and I sat up all one Friday night in the attic with Thermoses of coffee and sandwiches, and the portable telly. Nothing happened, of course, and all Flora's instruments – ghost hunters look for changes in magnetic energy and temperature and so on – remained completely steady, but it was fun. She was a kind of catalyst, who seemed to link Barley and me together; she had a lovely, grave face, and translucent skin and white, elegant hands and good legs, but I felt not a flicker of jealousy. I liked her too much. And so mostly because of Flora, Barley consented to do the programme and that was the end of us.

I heard that Flora went to Barley and Doris's wedding, and that disappointed me. But I suppose she was just one of the number who said, 'Oh, we don't take sides' and drifted off anyway.

'You shouldn't have told Doris Dubois that you were happy,'

said Dr Jamie Doom. I am back with Dr Doom. 'That was a red rag, if not to a bull, to a wounded cow. Poor Doris Dubois, she is very unhappy.'

I took a look at this man today, for the first time as if he were a human being, not a therapist. He is tall and broad and looks rather like a North London Harrison Ford. He keeps trying to make me love whom I hate and hate whom I love. Love Doris Dubois; hate Barley. He says I am perverse, but I think he's talking about himself. I feel oddly indifferent to Walter, at the moment, as if he didn't enter into any relevant equation. I hope proper feeling will return soon. I daresay I am still in shock. When I look inwards everything is jagged, the edges torn: it is hard to explain it to Dr Doom. I am wounded with too rough a sword.

After I'd been to see Dr Chandri, a spooky enough experience, which had left me with the notion in my head that I was literally growing younger: actually as well as emotionally and in the eyes of others – because what else was I to make of it? – I came home to find Walter was not there. I was too proud to call Doris's number, although Walter had left it there with me on his painting table amongst the tubes of paint and the rags and the smeared bottle of turpentine. He uses the expensive real stuff now I am with him, and no longer has to make do with the turps substitute the art students use. Ten o'clock came, eleven. Still no Walter. I drank a bottle of wine. I opened another. Midnight. Half past. Lady Juliet with her distorted face looked out at me from the easel. Walter had drawn a crude line around all her edges to slim her down to Doris Dubois. The Bulgari necklace, important and unalterable, sat serenely round the smooth neck, amidst paint mayhem.

*   *   *

Walter's portrait of me was now off the easel and on the wall. I did look good. Not sweet, like Lady Juliet, but somehow good. I took some comfort from it.

But I could no longer hide from myself that Doris and Walter must surely be doing more than talking about her portrait. Unless Walter had had an accident: but I knew from experience that an accident was the least likely thing. How many times, after Carmichael turned sixteen, had I not been onto the police, and the hospitals, reporting a lost child, to be met with a laugh and a don't worry, mother, he'll be doing what boys do, he'll be back. And so he was, with other boys, and I'd be worrying about Aids by then. Bonding is a terrible thing: whether it be the love of the mother for the child, or the woman for the man, it is no more than a life sentence in anxiety.

The phone rang. I rushed to it. Then held my hand. Let him wait, let him think I had gone to bed and was sleeping soundly when he deigned to call. It was not Walter, it was Doris Dubois on the phone. 'You'd better come round and fetch your Walter. He's lying here on my floor dead drunk.'

I went round in a taxi, beyond emotion, like an automaton, as one is when the worst befalls. And she was right, he was, and naked. And beside him were strewn Polaroid photographs of Doris Dubois, also naked.
'Just take him away,' said Doris Dubois, 'He's a terrible nuisance.'
'I'll tell Barley about this,' I said.
'About what?' she asked. Well yes, about what? About how Walter Wells was doing her portrait but got drunk and lost control and Doris had to call his girlfriend to take him away?

'These photographs,' I stumbled. Surely they added up to something.

'Good God, those photos are years back,' she trilled. 'I haven't worn my hair like that for years, all over my face.'

And she stared at me smirking from beneath a curtain of wild hair, defying me. And I just took Walter home. He drooped and lolled around and smelt of sick.

'She opened the door to me with nothing on,' he said, the next morning. 'I should have left straight away. But I was taken aback. And I don't fancy her one bit, I just thought here's this woman making a fool of herself, why doesn't she put her clothes back on? She talked about sending a team to my New York opening. After that I can't remember much,' he said. 'But how did I get so drunk? I was only drinking fizzy orange.'

And I believed him. Does it matter what a man does if he doesn't know what he's doing, if it's not in his consciousness later? It can hardly count as infidelity. At least, not rationally. I'm just shocked, still shocked, nothing seems quite real, except the memory of Doris Dubois laughing and victorious. I can see the attraction of evil. It is so sudden and complete and effective a destruction it leaves you breathless and laughing. Good is gradual and slow and dull and takes forever. You can unknit love in the twinkling of an eye, the emergence from nothing of a Polaroid portrait. I need time to build love up again: for event and laughter to put this incident in proper perspective.

Walter is back at his easel again, gritting his teeth, studying the tilt of Doris's eye, the curve of her lovely, popular, laughing mouth. What is he thinking about? Her? There is a bit of his life missing: just three hours or so, but like the memory on a computer perhaps there is no erasing it. You can get rid of it from your screen so you'll never have to see it again, you can set more memory free for use, but everything is still there on the hard disc.

Whatever happened in that room is recorded on the tape Harry Bountiful left with the porter at Tavington Court, but I will not listen to it. I do not want to know. I would rather trust Harry. It can stay in the porter's care.

Dr Jamie Doom – I am back with Dr Doom – says Doris Dubois wants to destroy me more than she wants to have Barley. I am the one she's out to get. It's me, not Barley, who is the focus of her attentions. It was just my bad luck to be the one in her steamroller path, to get crushed. She is the woman who goes round breaking up marriages, as she couldn't break up that of her parents'. She is the child who loves her father too much, and lusts after him, and hates her mother. *Why doesn't she just die? asks the girl child, so I can look after him, I would do it so much better than she does, I could love him so much better, and the guilt of that thought will stay with her always.* So Doris is doomed to go on repeating the pattern forever. As soon as I lose interest in Barley, as soon as I relinquish him, so will she. Already she's losing interest, or she wouldn't be bothering with Walter.

Poor Doris Dubois, says Dr Doom. As well pity a steamroller. Poor me, I say. He says it is the fate of all mothers to have a hard time from their daughters. How can I know? I only have a son, and I am sure Carmichael, though he backs out of the picture when the going gets rough, doesn't spend his life running off with other men's wives to spite his father because he loves me too much, he just spends his life hopelessly in love

139

with men who don't love him. To which Dr Doom would, no doubt, briskly reply: he's just recreating his childhood, trying to attract his father's attention and so on – so I don't even bother to discuss it with him. You can never win with therapists. Conscious of his duty to the Court, he asks a few questions to make sure I have no immediate intention of killing Doris Dubois, and that is the end of the session.

My fancy roams these days. I look at Dr Doom with a speculative eye and wonder what he'd be like in bed, what kind of children he'd make. I married Barley so young I suppose I never went through that stage, and have to do it now. Or else it's just a positive transference; everyone, he says, falls in love with their therapist at first. Well, bless me, do they then! 'Falling in love' means something very different to him than it does to me; to him it seems some quiet inclination, some gentle obsession. To me it's life-earthquake stuff. The negative transference – apparently also to be expected – to him is a mild dislike, an acid word: to me it's car-ramming murder.

Dr Jamie Doom poo-poos my notion that I'm getting younger by the week and my emotions therefore flow more freely. An agreeable fiction, he says; you always looked good, even in the most stressful moments during the break-up of your marriage. How placid and passive that sounds; something that just happens, like an ice floe coming apart. *The break-up of your marriage*. No-one's fault, hot weather or something. But it bloody was someone's fault, and I wish I'd managed to mow her down. I may yet.

29

10.15 a.m.

Flora Upchurch called Barley at his office, which was in Upper Brook Street, within walking distance of Claridges, and Barley offered to use his influence to get them a table at the Ivy for lunch. Surprisingly, he had a free lunch that day. It had been Sir Ronald's turn to cancel, but he read nothing sinister into that. These summonses from Downing Street came from time to time and had to be obeyed; the appointment had been remade for the following week, when both men were able to find a window in their schedules.

'Isn't the Ivy a bit public?' Flora asked, puzzling him a bit. What did she mean? Obviously there was nothing between him and Flora. She was like the daughter he and Grace should have had. And Doris wouldn't mind. It was a Wednesday. The show went out on Thursdays so Wednesday was Doris's really busy day, there was no way Doris could come too. Odd that Flora, on the show as well, could make a Wednesday lunch but no doubt she'd tell him all about it over Caesar salad or caramelised onion tart. He would have the latter, since it was

141

lunch with Flora, not with Doris. Then he'd probably choose the fishcakes.

Barley was happy to hear from Flora. Sometimes it was pleasant to be reminded of his past calm life with Grace, of the days when Wild Oats was all of a piece and called the Manor House, there was a familiar bed to go to, and the restful contours of a lifelong partner under the blankets. It was not that he had been actively unhappy with Grace, just bored. He had needed a woman with more vitality, more up and go, and had found one in Doris. When he had Grace, of course, he had been able to slip out from time to time to energise himself: now he had Doris he would not dare, but then why would he want to? Doris used up all available sexual energies and even a bit more; he would arrive at his office quite tired and that was not always a good thing. A good mood, yes, but one missed clues, rumours in the wind. Perhaps more sex at night, less in the morning, was the way to keep his edge.

It would be his birthday soon. One was as old as one felt, and he felt pretty young. He had Doris to thank for that. And she didn't make a fuss of birthdays the way Grace had, unnecessarily emphasising and publicising the passage of the years. Age was something you kept to yourself.

All the same, hearing Flora's soft voice, he had been vividly reminded of the night they'd all stayed up ghost hunting, with coffee and sandwiches. A sudden happy painful memory. Grace's soft thigh pressed up against his in the dark, and her whispery laughter, a sudden renewal of sexual interest that surprised him. But without Flora as catalyst it wouldn't have happened. A marriage that needed a third person around to bring it to life couldn't be all that good. And shortly after that

142

he appeared on Doris's show and he and she had got together, and that was that. And Flora had come along to the wedding, and looked very good and cheerful, so he assumed she thought the formalisation of the union was a good thing, and was on his side in the divorce, not that sides needed to be taken, or not until Grace had put herself out of court – or into it, as it happened – trying to mow poor Doris down in the Jaguar, which had shocked and upset her no end. Doris was not as tough as she looked. Grace always had been a rotten driver: couldn't even drive straight enough to get Doris. Doris was smooth, flawless and confident at the wheel. He loved being driven by her. He must call up Bulgari and see how the necklace was getting on. He'd have to move funds about a bit when the time came: the portion in the Cayman Islands would have to be released. He'd manage. He always had. Well, mostly.

Lunch with Flora, without Grace. He had never had to worry about the possibility of Grace being unfaithful. It had simply not been in her nature, though once she was on her own it was remarkable how soon she'd shacked up with someone else. That hurt him, rather. He could see infidelity might well be in Doris's impulsive nature, but she was too busy; when would she find the time for extra-marital adventure, and why should she want to? Was not he, the great Barley Salt, more than enough to fill heart, mind and body? Thank God the unfortunate episode of the morning before hadn't rattled her, nor indeed him. Just as the mere thought of the sleeping pills in the bathroom cupboard, there to be taken in an emergency, can be enough to induce a good night's sleep, so the awareness of Viagra, just a doctor's prescription away, gave sexual confidence.

Onion tart, fishcakes. He'd have a helping of fat chips too,

143

with mayonnaise. And wine, yes, the Californian. He'd always drunk French until Doris came along and gave him confidence.

11.10 a.m.

A friendly phone call from a member of the Government. Barley was not to worry, if he was worrying. Opera Noughtie was too favourite a Government project for it to be abandoned. Although the swing was towards Science and Decommissioning away from the Arts, which meant Billyboy Justice's Millennium Cleanup project was looking distinctly bullish, it was more likely to find a site in Wales than Scotland. There was now some talk of combining the all-European lewisite operation with the overdue Sellafield cleanup, and the very word nuclear was a red rag to an Argyle bull. Opera might induce yawns up and down the Firth of Forth but singing was at least safe. It never did a regime down South any good to stir up the Picts in the North; they rumbled away with their discontent at the best of times, no-one wanted them actually to boil over.

Barley's PA called Harrods and had them send a dozen bottles of a rather acceptable single-malt to his contact in the Government – for Christmas. Normally Barley would have asked the bloke down to the country for the weekend, but that was out of the question at the moment.

11.20 a.m.

A message from reception. Could his chauffeur – Ross – have a minute of his time? Barley hoped there was not trouble with Doris, who had it in for Ross. She wanted some slim young thing to drive them round, it seemed. She didn't like Ross's looks, his accent, his dandruff, his belly. Now there was some business of making Ross weigh in every Friday: a management technique, Barley suspected. You set up some plausible, but near impossible task in the apparent interest of the employee, and when the latter fails to deliver you have a good answer ready for the unfair dismissal tribunal.

Doris complained Ross was on Grace's side. Barley didn't think Ross cared two hoots who sat beside Barley in the back, though he did sometimes transmit a certain antagonism through his broad-shouldered back. Ross saw his job as driving Barley around, and was loyal to his employer. He was on Barley's side. Though now Doris had taken over the staff, saying Barley was too soft and paid too much and employees only despised you for it, she had already cost him one PA, three gardeners and one maid. Barley did not want Ross to go. Ross knew every rat run in London, and how to get out of trouble in a hurry; a chauffeur who doubled as a bodyguard was the thing to have, these days. Barley would have to have a word with Doris about this.

Ross was shown in, and said he was handing in his notice. He had weighed himself at the Health Club which the former Mrs Salt had recommended, and now that Doris had made him go on a diet he had put on three pounds. No, there was nothing wrong with the scales; they belonged to the Health Club. He had been offered another job, with a detective agency. Barley prevailed upon him to stay until the end of the year. Ross, who was almost tearful, agreed.

11.40 a.m.
Doris calls. 'Just to say I love you, and we've a terrific show tonight. I've seen the Leadbetter clips' – Leadbetter was all set to win the Turner with a trompe-l'oeil painting in a frame made

145

of compacted sewage of the kind they fed to turkeys in France – 'and they're fantastic: they let us film him in drag! The guy works in Blahnik heels . . .'

'Doris,' said Barley, 'I've just had Ross up here in my office. He's handing in his notice. I don't want that. I like him.'

'He's too fat,' said Doris. 'Too twentieth-century. We deserve better than Ross.'

'I'm dealing with the Russians, Doris. I need a bodyguard.' He wondered if he really did. The Opera Noughtie scheme was going to go through, but it could do no harm to impress upon Doris the kind of man she was with.

'Good God,' said Doris. 'Ross's so slow on his feet he couldn't get a cow with a Kalashnikov.'

He wondered if she were taking drugs. But she couldn't be, could she? She said they didn't agree with her.

'He's agreed to stay to the end of the year,' said Barley. 'I don't want any more of these weigh-ins.'

'That's okay then,' said Doris brightly. 'So long as he goes at the end of the year. My, we are serious today.'

He forgot to tell her he was lunching with Flora.

11.45 a.m.–12.15 p.m.

Phone calls from various contacts in the building world, architects and engineers, wanting contracts, offering work. Business was brisk out there. Office buildings and arts complexes springing into life all over the city, all over the country. And bridges, but the less said about them the better. Thank God he'd had nothing to do with that project. These periods of brisk economic activity – he'd been told they coincided with sunspots – were once marked by the urgent pinging of fax machines all over the building, but now there was an eerie hush: communication was by the swift silent transmission of e-mail through virtual space. Twenty of them waiting on his machine – they could wait – and probably about fifty straight through to his PA.

He'd be happier if he'd got the foundations for Opera Noughtie actually into the ground six months back. He hated this stage of things, when all other funds were in place and you had to wait for the green light for matching subsidies from the State. At least in this country the government only changed by way of election, not by coup.

He never touched a project in Africa, or in Polynesia.

12.30 p.m.
A phone call from Miranda in reception.
'There's a young lady to see you. Well, not exactly young. I'm not sure what she wants, but she says it's personal.'
'I'm just out to lunch at the Ivy.'
'Oh! She's taken the lift up, she's on her way. I'm sorry, sir, I couldn't stop her. She's left her shopping bag behind.'
'That's okay, I'll deal with her.'

She was called Natasha. She looked young enough to Barley. She had a plump high bosom and a tiny belted waist, long thin legs, gold sandals with very high heels, and a mass of reddish-gold curls. She spoke very bad English very fast. She started to unbutton her white lacey blouse even as she came in, to display patches of rather brownish freckled bosom. Barley was too startled to lift the phone and call for help. She said she had been sent by her friend Mr Makarov to see if there was any way in which she could assist Barley. He had a spare lunch hour, she knew.

Makarov? Familiar, but not all that familiar. Hadn't there been

147

someone of that name at Lady Juliet's charity auction? The one at which Grace had gone off with the painter? Someone standing next to Billyboy Justice? Things were going on here that shouldn't be. A blatant honey trap. Once these were confined to Moscow hotels with bulky KGB cameras in the chandeliers: now they had moved to London and the cameras and microphones were so miniaturised they fitted into the underwire of the bra and the elastic of the knickers. How did she know his lunch date had cancelled?

He shooed her out before she could disrobe any further and she left her card, pouting and biting her plump lip.

12.45 p.m.
When he went down to reception Miranda was giggling. Miranda was on a state-subsidised youth-employment scheme. That is to say she worked for free, while the government paid her the dole. He would offer her a proper job, he thought. She was bright and funny and eager, though she was spotty, spoke badly and couldn't spell. At least she washed her hair sometimes which was more than many of the job applicants did, and it flowed fluffily around, and didn't hang dankly.

Together they looked in the Selfridges bags Natasha had left. Twenty pairs of transparent net panties and matching bras in red and gold spots, twenty pairs in leopard-skin, twenty in orange patterned with blue fish. Twenty leather thongs.
'She'll be back for them, when she remembers,' said Miranda. 'Yuk.'
'I think they're rather good,' said Barley, but then he would. 'But why twenty?'
'It's an invasion,' said Miranda. 'Perhaps the other girls are too busy to shop for themselves. Fat chance we English have;

148

we've got to sit at desks, how else to earn a living now they're over here.'

Barley decided that he had probably not been singled out for individual attention, that he'd misheard the name Makorksy, that there was nothing sinister in the fact that the woman knew he was free for lunch, or would have been if Flora hadn't called by chance – many men, thus propositioned, would have cancelled any appointment there and then – and went off light-hearted to the Ivy for lunch. He was indeed tired, morally and mentally as well as physically.

30

'Grace,' said Walter to his loved one, 'if you were to look at me as a stranger would, how old would you say I was?'

'About forty,' she said, 'but I'm very bad at ages.' It was evening. The nights had closed in. Rain and wind battered against the windowpane. They were cosy together, and whatever had happened at Doris's apartment now made them laugh, not weep. How quickly women forget, and men too. A life that seems intolerable one day, the next seems quite passable, at least if sex is there to provide a united front against life.

Without it, couples quickly spring apart and resume their separate identities. To be separate is perhaps a nobler aim, but to be united, as St Paul might have said, was at least better than to burn.

Doris's face on the easel was nearly finished now, and sat rather oddly and thinly on Lady Juliet's robust body. Walter would turn his attention to narrowing the figure presently. He would move the background in and fuzzy up its edges a little: he liked the idea of substituting a white and blue streaked background for the solid blue it now was, but seemed to remember, though he could not be quite sure, Doris saying she wanted the portrait wholly unchanged, other than what she called the two significants: Lady Juliet's head must become hers, and she herself must be seen as no more than a size ten, an eight if possible. He told Grace he felt obliged to obey.

'You have your artistic integrity,' Grace protested. 'You have your reputation to consider.'

'I compromised those when I accepted this commission in the first place,' said Walter. 'What painter in his right mind takes on this kind of duff job?'

'Goya,' she replied, smartly, and that made him feel better. When a new patron beats upon the gates, it is wisest for artists to express their enthusiasm, and there is honour in the custom. Integrity is what you can afford. He decided not to worry about it. Things were going well otherwise. The Manhatt. had told him that a British film company had been in touch, wanting to film the private view if dates could be arranged. He wondered what film company that could be; he'd get back to the Gallery and ask them.

'We'll be rich!' cried Grace. In her head her money was his money, so his was hers. As long as he wasn't too proud how happy they could be.

But the Manhatt., he warned her, would take fifty per cent of the wall price, the Bloomsday would want their cut, his agent would take fifteen per cent, and Inland Revenue would be taking twenty-five per cent if he sold a few, and forty per cent if he sold any more, so no, he would not be rich. You only got rich when your paintings got above the £10,000 mark. But he might become respected. He wanted respect. He did not like being patronised. He did not like being young. He wanted to cease to be seen as an Outsider in the Young Art Scene, and become an Insider in the Established Art Scene, where he and his paintings would be much more comfortable.

'You look serious enough already,' she said. 'Standing in that light you could just about pass for forty.'

'That's good,' he said. 'Forty's good. But I wouldn't want to get any older.'

'I don't want to get much younger,' she said. 'It's too unsettling.'

'We're not really, are we?' he asked. 'It is all in our heads.'

She picked out another grey hair from his head. His eyebrows had got noticeably shaggier. Her period had started. Every now and then she had to clutch her stomach and take aspirin. Supposing she got pregnant?

'Of course it's all in our heads.'

Doris, though her head still perched a little oddly, and Walter would have to see to that, smiled down at them quite pleasantly, as once had Lady Juliet. Grace had prevailed upon Walter to paint her in as kindly a fashion as he could, bearing in mind how she was born, not how she had become. How Doris would have been, according to Dr Jamie Doom, had she not fallen in love with her father one day, and learned to hate her mother and all wives thereafter. It had been quite difficult to persuade Walter, but she'd managed it.

'We are put here in this world to sop up evil,' Grace earnestly explained to him. 'We must see ourselves as scavengers of good and find the best in everything, even Doris.'

She even stopped him adding boiled linseed oil to the paint, so that Doris's head would turn black in a hundred years' time. At least he had proper turps now, and not the cheaper substitute that he'd used on the layers underneath. But was there something different about the new batch of paint which Walter had bought? Because on occasion when they got up in the mornings the new paint would have failed to hold properly on its base and a little would have slipped and slid, even cracked, so as to pull down the edges of Doris's mouth, or slant her eyes, and make her look not quite so nice. The effect was quite other than Walter's earlier attempt at light-hearted caricature using acrylics on oil-varnish glaze, and now overpainted: it had an unsettling, slightly hideous new quality to it.

Walter called the paint manufacturers on the phone, who insisted that no-one else had complained, and that their product was not at fault; they superciliously suggested that the canvas might not have been properly prepared. So Walter just painted over to cover up the damage and hoped to God the varnish he'd use when everything was finished would do the job, and keep Doris's face in one place.

Grace confessed to Walter that she'd had his meeting with Doris Dubois taped by Harry Bountiful, and at first he was angry, as he had every right to be. Then he laughed and said when they had the courage they would both go round together to Tavington Court and hear what the tape had to say, and his lost hours be restored to him.

31

Flora was looking pale but very beautiful and rather angry. She wore a little flowered skirt and a flimsy jumper and a string of pearls and arrived at the Ivy without a coat. She shivered a little over the Caesar salad; but soon warmed up and her cheeks even grew a bit pink with animation. She knew so much about so many obscure things to do with history, culture and art it used to leave Barley stumped. But he was catching up, thanks to Doris.

In the four month gap between Doris sending in Flora to do the research for the show in which Barley was to feature and the actual taping of the programme Barley had come to realise just how inadequate, uneducated and ignorant he was. Talk of Brunelleschi or the Van Eycks, or Medici patronage and Barley had no idea what anyone was going on about, or even what century. Grace never had much of a clue but knew a bit more than Barley did: and that had disconcerted him too. Who was Savonarola? Some kind of salami sausage, Barley thought. But no. Some religious geezer way back then. Flora knew, Doris knew. Grace guessed but got it wrong: she thought he was some kind of Marxist philosopher. Barley just made a fool of himself.

One of the reasons he had married Doris, Barley didn't deny it, was to rid himself of the feeling that he was not the equal of the architects, the politicians, the planners with whom he dealt daily and who had all been to University, many even to Oxford or Cambridge. Sure, Barley had the knack of making money at a level that they for the most part did not, but they mysteriously won more of the world's respect and he wanted part of it.

He was not ready to hear Doris criticised – she was his wife, after all – and to her credit Flora did not indulge her obvious anger. She told him over the croutons that she had been fired by Doris, and was now unemployed.

'She is quite good at firing people,' said Barley, cautiously. 'It's her strength. She even got Grace fired,' and he laughed a little. He asked Flora what the reason was: there must be some kind of reason. She must have done something wrong. Even Ross had refused to lose weight; if he'd had any self-discipline he would have lost at least a pound or so. So what was it?

'I wore a white dress to your wedding and my legs are better than hers,' said Flora promptly. 'I upstaged the bride.'

Barley automatically looked down to see if they were – she had them rather fetchingly tucked round the feet of her chair – and it was true they were supple and shapely, with perhaps a little more flesh around the calf than Doris sported. Doris's legs were very long, but a little too thin for perfection. And Flora had delightful knees.

'Oh come off it,' said Barley. 'That's stupid talk.'

'And you looked at me too long,' said Flora, 'and she caught you at it.'

155

'You just looked so nice,' said Barley helplessly. 'Why now, then? If you're right and this is the reason, why has she waited until now to pounce?'

'Because she thought she'd found someone else to do the job,' said Flora. 'Only she hasn't. Jasmine Orbachle. I went to art college with her. She works at Bulgari now, but before that she was doing research on ancient jewellery. I've warned her off so now she's staying put and that means Doris doesn't have anyone.'

'Oh dear,' said Barley. It was difficult to know what side he was on. 'That's bad.'

'It is particularly bad,' said Flora, 'because of the Leadbetter business coming up. The show's backing Leadbetter to get the Turner and he simply isn't going to. The public have gone right off all that Culture of Disgust stuff. The critics will follow like lambs. There's going to be a seismic shift and Doris will have three whole programmes in the can about yuck art.'

'The show's allowed to make a mistake sometimes,' said Barley. 'It's normally spot-on. It's famous for it.'

'Because of me,' said Flora. 'Not because of Doris. Doris is good at knowing everyone who's anyone in the art world but she can't tell a good painting from the back of a bus. She's dreadfully insecure, you know.'

Barley's mouth fell open. A waiter asked if everything was all right. He said it was. 'The knives are out for her,' said Flora. 'In the end you can make too many enemies. She's not the only one just waiting for an excuse to fire people. The thing is, she needs me, and I want you to tell her so. For her sake: because you can get quite fond of Doris even though she is a monster.'

Barley said he knew that. Flora said it was strange how and why you loved and liked people: it was seldom because they were good. Except for a few people like Grace. She had wept buckets when the marriage split up, and had been to see Grace in prison but Grace wouldn't see her.

'She did a lot of not seeing people,' said Barley.

'I pray for her,' said Flora.

'Keep it up,' said Barley. 'Because I reckon she's quite happy.' He would have liked Flora to pray for him too but felt too embarrassed to say so. He felt like crying, which was not what grown men in the Ivy often did. There was a table a couple along at which were sitting four new peers of the Realm, from the worlds of art, architecture, opera and cultural television. They were drinking pink champagne – a magnum – and seemed very cheerful. He thought they might well not be if the rumours about the new ascendency of Science were true. But they waved happily at Barley, who had met all of them at many a meeting about Opera Noughtie. He waved agreeably back. No doubt they thought Flora was his mistress. Too bad. The women the Lords were with tended not to spend too much time on their appearance. They wore long drippy flat clothes: much as they would have done in the Sixties. The miniskirt had simply passed them by while they thought of more important things. Very few women got it right. Grace felt easy in clothes which would have suited a vicarage garden back in the Fifties. Doris's were whatever *Tatler* said they should be. Flora's face was way back in Medici times, so far back it made her pale, but her clothes and her style were of the effortless Now. He liked that. And her wrists were so thin.

32

Ethel Handy is thirty-nine, or so she says. She has a neat small-featured face and dark short hair. She looks competent and is good at figures. She wears tidy blouses and well-fitting skirts. She embezzled £80,000 from her employers, a chain of bookmakers and got three years when discovered. She was trying to pay off her mortgage and a man who was blackmailing her about some rude photographs taken when she was sixteen, which he threatened to show her aged parents. He had been the photographer. She thought her employers exploited both her and the public. She thought that if she gave him what he wanted he would go away, but he didn't. He went to the police about the fraud and vanished with her best friend and the money. The mortgage company foreclosed. She was sentenced to three years inside. The prison authorities were more soft-hearted than the judge and gave her as many privileges as they could.

When I was in prison Ethel was a good friend. She stood between me and the other girls. Grace can't help speaking the way she does, she'd tell them. She's a doctor's daughter.

She can't help crying. She loves her husband and her husband ditched her. Yes, she's the woman in the papers who tried to murder the husband's mistress. No, she doesn't want drugs. It's not her fault Sandy (one of the women guards) fancies her. She doesn't like being touched up either, she just doesn't spit and snarl like the rest of you animals. No, Grace, if it's Lancaster Stew on the menu don't have it, someone once found a sheep's eye in it, take the vegetarian instead. No, she's not going to give her visitors letters to take out of the prison. Her visitors get searched just like anyone else.

I owe Ethel.

Ethel nurtured me and answered for me until my wits were back and I stopped the weeping, which was when, on Ethel's advice, I stopped taking the tranquillisers. We were locked up in our cells for sometimes seventeen or eighteen hours a day. The trick was, I learned, to think in terms of 'we' not 'me', and the authorities as 'them'. The attempt to see yourself as apart, as some kind of specially sensitive and innocent victim of circumstances, was pointless. I'd been in with the M and M's, the murderers and molesters, the really spooky ones, for a couple of weeks, but they must have decided I was harmless and moved me out of that wing and in with the petty offenders, the ones who'd been through the magistrates' courts, not the High Courts: forty-year-olds in for brawling and seventeen-year-olds for shop-lifting lipsticks: lots for drug offences, and one seventeen-year-old with a month-old baby now in care, in for three months for stealing a prawn cocktail. *'The magistrate had it in for me: I had him in the back of a car once, the filthy mean old git.'* We could look at TV, I got to know Richard and Judy well. We could go to cookery and childcare classes: everyone did their best but the sum of any institution is always worse than the sum of its parts. The place smelt of urine and disinfectant and was never quiet: even at three in the morning sudden animal shrieks and bellows and wails would shake the air, born of rage or despair. There was a male guard everyone hated who did random strip-searching: he had a fleshy face and piggy eyes and a slack body and he'd look at us with contempt and desire, both. Ethel said, 'Think of him with no clothes on,' which made me giggle. I owe Ethel all right.

All the same. When Walter and I went round to Tavington Road and asked Mr Zeigler for Harry Bountiful's tape of Walter's encounter with Doris he said he'd given it to Ethel to take round to me. And there was no sign of Ethel in the flat or out of it, and her suitcase was gone. And Walter said sadly he supposed she'd use it for blackmail. I'd rashly told Ethel the story of Walter, Lady Juliet, the portrait and the Bulgari jewels of Doris's desire. She had seen the portrait on the easel. And of course she already knew about Barley and Doris Dubois, from the time when we were both in prison and frankly I could talk about little else. She had told me that the cure for one man is another man and she had been right. Embezzler and fraudster Ethel might be, and an outcast of society, but she was wise and, I had thought, good.
'She won't do that to me,' I said. 'Not Ethel. She's my friend.'
'Oh yes she would,' said Walter. 'I know life, I know what people do. If they pray not to be led into temptation, it's because temptation is what they can't resist. My father told me that.'
'Oh Walter,' I said. 'You sound so old. Just like your father.'
'And you're so young and full of hope,' he said, rather dryly. And I could see that if it went on like this I would lose him. He needed me to be worldly-wise.

33

'Doris, listen to me,' said Barley to Doris over breakfast at Claridges. He had insisted on bacon and eggs with fried bread, sausages and tomatoes. She was horrified, but he said he had a hard day in front of him. Breakfast arrived, not on a large tray but on a trolley with heated plates and metal covers, which had to be wheeled into the room and served by waiters. 'Are you really going on with this Leadbetter business? Because I have reason to believe he isn't going to win the Turner Prize, and you like me can afford to be wrong about a few things but not about everything. Just don't enthuse too wildly about him.'

She studied him from beneath her fringe of wild hair. She had not had it cut recently. 'Barley,' she said. 'You know one or two things about art since I have taken you in hand, but not enough to know this. Who have you been speaking to? It could be that bitch Lady Juliet, who hates me; it could be your ex-wife Grace who's shacked up with next year's winner, Walter Wells. Or it could be Flora Upchurch.'

'It's none of these people,' he said, but she was not a good person to lie to. He had lied to Grace with impunity, and though she had often known he was lying, she had usually been prepared to accept his judgement, that the lie would do less harm than the truth. Grace could tolerate what Doris could not, that we all move in a world full of less than perfect solutions, of least worst options.

Doris yawned in a languorous way and said, 'Darling, I know perfectly well that you had lunch with Flora at the Ivy, and that you chose not to tell me about it.'
And instead of being angry, and barely waiting for the last of the room-service staff to leave, she dragged him to the bed and was so enthusiastic and sudden in her lovemaking that he did not have time to be apprehensive, and performed to her evident satisfaction, and his own great relief, before he had time to think, or worry.
'How did you know?' he asked.
'No-one goes to the Ivy for secrecy,' she said. 'They go to be seen.'
'Flora only wanted me to warn you about Leadbetter,' Barley said.
'No she didn't,' said Doris. 'She wants her job back. Well, she can have it.'

Afterwards she wanted to go down to Bulgari to hurry them up about her necklace, but Barley, emboldened by his protein and fat-rich breakfast, said he couldn't spare the time, and added as an afterthought that she was not to go down there to give Jasmine Orbachle a hard time.
'Otherwise what?' asked Doris, eyes narrowed.
'Otherwise nothing,' said Barley, prudently, thinking he had got away with quite enough for one day, and so he had.

Doris went straight to the studio instead of spending the morning on the phone and shopping, which put her in a bad mood. When she got to reception there were two visitors waiting to see her. A plain, spotty woman who had obviously nothing to do with the arts or the media, and a rather glam man from abroad with a camel hair suit and a gold tiepin in the shape of Concorde. They introduced themselves as Ethel and Hashim and said they would like a word with her in private. Doris said she was very, very busy and perhaps they could make an appointment. They said no, it was in her interest to see them now. They were wearing the security badges given out at the front desk so Doris assumed they had at least some kind of clearance. She took them through into the studio, and on to the set. She had found in the past that if you spoke to bailiffs – her spending habits had in the past led her into some financial difficulty – on set, that is to say in the world according to TV, with its great dim-vaulted ceilings above slung with gantries, its brilliant, hot artificial lights below, duck-boarded electrical cables tripping up the unwary, and then (cynosure of all eyes) the glowing harmonies of the set itself: the glossy table, unnaturally clean, the comfortable armchairs, and the sense of the whole world watching – that they lost the thread of what they were after, and would often simply stumble from the place in search of reality and sanity, leaving Doris in peace.

She had a feeling that these two betokened trouble, though exactly what she could not be sure. Perhaps to do with something going on at Wild Oats? The architect and designer were balking at the deadline of December twelfth, now only two weeks away, and she had made her lawyer write stiff letters to them, explaining in no uncertain terms that according to the terms of their contract – yes, certainly in the small print, but surely they read the small print? She always did – if they did not finish in time they would get no more money at all from her, and would be obliged to remit such funds as she had already

163

paid over to them. And that since also, under the terms of the contract, if they brought in new builders they were obliged to pay any excess from their own pockets, they would be best advised to put pressure on Belgradia Builders to deliver.

Barley was going to be sixty on the twelfth of December and she loved Barley and would give him a birthday to remember.

But her horoscope in the *Daily Mail* had warned her against any extreme action in defence of the righteousness of her cause, saying the velvet glove was always better than the iron fist, and though Doris had never before found this to be the case, she rather trusted the *Mail*'s astrologer and so was going a little prudently. She was hopping mad about Jasmine letting her down and pretty sure that Flora had had a hand in it, and totally enraged that Barley had taken Flora to the Ivy so sneakily but she had been very velvet-gloved about it all.

Had she not? The *Mail* would be proud of her. And she would be velvet-gloved with this pair too. People out of the blue, events that surprised you, were often sent by Fate, she found, either for good or bad. The Bulgari people had stood out against her wishes, which had certainly surprised her, but see how it had led to her encounter with Walter Wells and the revenge on Lady Juliet which she had in mind. If you couldn't achieve an effect one way you could in another. She must remember to confirm with the Manhatt. Gallery that they would be there to film a week before Christmas. She kept her promises. Walter Wells would be famous by next Spring, and as enamoured of her, Doris, as Barley had ever been. She would see how the Opera Noughtie project worked out before she decided whether or not to keep Barley on as a husband.

These days it didn't do to be seen to have affairs: this was the age of openness, secrecy was a no-no. You could achieve legitimacy in your sex life, and variety as well, so long as you paid off the lawyers.

'This is Hashim,' said the one who called herself Ethel. She looked vaguely familiar. 'He is a member of the Royal Family of Jordan. He is descended from the Hashemites, from which the word assassin comes.'

'How very interesting,' said Doris, casually. Did he carry a knife, a gun? 'I did a programme on the art treasures of Jordan once, and quite magnificent they were. How can I help you?'

'We'd like you to listen to this tape,' said Ethel. 'I expect with all this equipment about you can sort that out. It's a tape of you and Walter Wells having a conversation, well, kind of, with you making all the running, and I don't think you'd want your bosses to hear it. Or your nice new husband, for that matter.'

'I see,' said Doris, thinking fast. Her flat was bugged. Why? How? Who? It was routine enough for new-anchors and political correspondents, and no-one cared much, but arts presenters did not usually warrant such attention. Probably a private matter.

Grace? Possibly. Well, an eavesdropper hears no good of themselves. And at least she had got the old bat to sit up and take notice of something.

'How much do you want for it?'

No point in beating about the bush. Barley would probably pay up, anyway. If the worst came to the worst she could accuse him of fancying Flora and say she was driven into someone else's arms by her extreme distress. Actually, she would hate it if there was anything going on, really hate it. She probably did love Barley, just a bit. It was odd how these things crept up on you. She could do so much more for Barley than Grace ever could. Why couldn't Grace just accept it?

Hashim shifted in his deep armchair, the one designed to make guests feel helpless, and the gold of his Concorde tiepin caught the light and glittered. If he had been a guest Make-Up would have asked him to remove it before the show. But he wasn't a guest, he was a blackmailer. Sometimes it was a little difficult to remember what was real life and what was studio, and when one intruded into the other like this you could feel a trifle disoriented yourself. He was sweating a little, his dark eyes unreadable. She hoped he was emotionally stable.

Ethel was more sensible: she perched on the edge of her chair ready to take off at any minute and didn't sink back into it, as he did. Trust a man. She didn't think they could have got through security if they had guns or knives; the metal detector would have picked them up, but they were a bit dozy downstairs and who would like to stop a man with a gold Concorde tiepin if he walked round it not through it. The rich can pass through the eye of security more easily than the poor. And the Ethel creature could easily pass herself off as someone in accounts, and get waved through. She might even *be* in accounts, which could explain both why she looked familiar and had got through the checks. Personally Doris wouldn't trust her further than she would throw her – not far, because she was a good size fourteen – she was just the kind of mousy type who runs off with the Pensioners' Social Fund to go on some ghastly holiday in the Bahamas. That being the sum of her aspirations.

Ah-hah! Ethel Handy, of course she'd looked familiar. In all the newspapers a couple of years back. Headlines because of what the Judge had said: Lord Longue, the same Judge as had tried Grace for trying to kill her: '*Much as I pity you, today's woman should be able to stand firm against blackmail. There is nothing to be ashamed of in nudity. It is something to be proud of.*' Well, unless you were a size twelve or above. But it had given the feature writers a field day. What is there left to hide? That you'd pay good money to hide?

'We don't want money,' said the convicted fraudster, now. What little squinny eyes she had, poor thing. 'All we want is for you to leave Walter Wells alone. You do anything more to upset my friend Grace and we're broadcasting this on the Internet, with copies to the regular newspapers. They'll love it.' Doris stretched out a hand to grab the tape. She couldn't stop herself.

'You're welcome to it,' said Ethel. 'We've got lots of copies back home. In fact we'd like you to keep this one. What was in the fizzy orange? Rohypnol?'

'What was it Judge Tobias Longue said?' asked Doris, in control of herself again, and she leant back in her chair with her hands clasped behind her neck, as if unafraid of any attack. Body language was always important. '"*Today's woman should stand firm against blackmail?*" He was quite right. She should. And I will. Do your worst. Broadcast and be damned.'

She was gratified to see Ethel looking mortified.

'It's the way they say,' said Doris, openly yawning. Attack is the best form of defence. 'A prison sentence doesn't stop when the gates clang open. Poor Ethel.' She smiled at Hashim. 'Did you know your friend was a jailbird? Four years for a truly mean fraud? I hope the tiepin isn't real because she's only after one thing. Money. You'd better look after yourself. She's a monster.'

*   *   *

But now the pair of them were looking around as though searching for escape, scared, blinded by spot lights, which suddenly now, in emergency mode, illuminated every corner of the studio. The alarm was sounding outside in the corridor. It made a terrible racket. Doris hoped there was nothing going out live in any of the other studio suites; no amount of soundproofing would help. Outside men were shouting.

Hashim had lurched headfirst out of his chair, and was on his feet and pulling Ethel after him: they were making for the Emergency Exit behind the velvet curtains which framed the set, clanging its old-fashioned metal bar open, grating the door closed behind them. That's a fast runner, she thought. Jordan Royals don't run like that. Only criminals and con men.
'They went that a-way,' she said, pointing to the other Exit, the one Hashim and Ethel had not used. She didn't know why, she suddenly had a fellow-feeling for them.

34

Carmichael asked Mr Zeigler where he could find his Mum. Mr Zeigler huffed and puffed and said there was a girl called McNab in Flat No. 32 on the third floor but no-one of that name who would be Carmichael's mother.

'Could be your sister, I suppose,' he said. 'She's in there now with her feller, won't be too happy to be disturbed, I warn you. All this coming and going, more men going into that apartment than ever come out of it. People leaving packages, God knows what, drugs, child porn? Don't blame me if I get rid of them as soon as I can. People get killed for less. There was a knifing round the corner only the other day.'

'I suppose she could still be using her married name,' said Carmichael, 'though she wrote to me that she wasn't now. Grace Salt?'

'That's the woman who did the murder,' said Mr Zeigler. 'In the newspapers. The landlords would draw the line at that. Mind you, these days anything goes. I'm just the one out in the front line, they don't think about that. Sitting here facing that door all day. Any nut could walk in off the street. No! No-one here called Salt.'

'I'll try Number 32,' said Carmichael. He patted the trembling old hand and was rewarded with a limpid, eager smile, which he ignored.

It had not occurred to him that his mother might not be here. He should have called and let her know he was coming. But he liked the *imprévu*, and to be impetuous, and he didn't want to spoil the surprise. Face to face was so much easier. He should have come over for the trial but he didn't want his name in the papers. He should have visited her in prison, of course he should, but his therapist had said cut the ties that bind, you're in a new world, you've got a new life, everyone deserves to be able to start again. And you shouldn't miss your appointments just at this juncture in your treatment. It was only when the treatment drifted towards the suggestion that his homosexuality was more an acting out, a defiance of his father, than an innate state of being, and the realisation dawned that the creep was a) homophobic and b) in love with Carmichael, that he broke free and began to use his own judgement.

He was now with Toby, a stage designer, but Toby was in New Zealand staging a massive theatrical show for some Berlin architect which involved tying up Mount Cook, the damaged volcano, in strands of hand-plaited Maori flax, or some such thing, while acting out Riwi's Last Stand below, and Carmichael had felt the need for London again and took Air Japan out of there for a break. Just a couple of weeks. He reckoned Toby could be faithful that long, but he wouldn't risk it much longer. He was a bit too zonked by jet lag to worry any more, in any case.

He knocked on the door of No. 32. And again. He could

hear movement inside. He gave in and rang the bell. A good old-fashioned echoey ring, that was something. Carmichael was always reluctant to press bell-pushes, for fear of hearing chimes, which got on his nerves terribly. In some respects, he could see, he was like his father, who preferred everything to be plain, sensible and straightforward. How Barley had got muddled up with Doris Dubois, God alone knew. The other mistresses had been of the classic bad-girl type, suffering alone over Christmas and holidays, in the end demanding marriage, at the first whiff of which request Barley had dumped them. Or else they got fed up and moved on to better prospects. Three concurrent girlfriends had gone just after Carmichael had taken his A-levels.

'Not until the boy's got through his exams,' Barley would say to them. 'I can't risk upsetting him.' Before A-levels it had been SATS, then GCSEs: for others who came later it would be Carmichael's BA, then his Master's, at the London School of Embroidery. And Doris Dubois had made it there after all others had failed. Perhaps only because Carmichael had gone to Australia, so that there were no further procrastinating excuses that Barley could offer. His Dad's remarriage was in a way Carmichael's fault. If only he could have stayed a boy forever.

It was an older brother of his schoolfriend Clive, Wentworth by name, who'd tapped Barley's office phone early on, thus providing the younger boys with hours of innocent pleasure. The tap was keyed to pick up only women's voices at a certain pitch. Had Barley only been gay, as Clive pointed out, Barley would have been spared the intrusion. Wentworth was a computer nerd and now on various Internet regulating bodies. Clive was in industrial design.

*   *   *

The door was opened by a young woman, recently out of bed, thick hair mussed, bare footed and wearing a man's rather well-washed black shirt. The colour was good but the fabric defeated.

'I'm sorry to disturb you,' said Carmichael. 'I'm looking for a Miss McNab. This is the number she gave me. She must have got it wrong.'

'Carmichael darling!' cried the young woman, and threw her arms around him.

'Mother?' asked Carmichael, and he could see that it was she. At any rate there was a photograph of him aged three on a beach with a woman who looked remarkably like this one.

She drew him into the flat saying he should have warned her, supposing she hadn't been there, she was hardly ever here these days and Mr Zeigler couldn't seem to keep anything in his head any more. He only ever did what was easiest. She supposed that's what people did when they got to be old.

'Have you had cosmetic surgery, Mum,' Carmichael asked. 'Or is that a wig, or what? What's going on round here?'

'Please don't say that kind of thing, Carmichael,' she begged. 'I don't know what to think. At first we thought it was just happiness, but when you open the door to your own son and he doesn't recognise you – Carmichael you're looking wonderful yourself, bronze and square and not in the least limpid.' He let that last go. She went on. 'Carmichael, we have a terrible feeling, Walter and I, that I'm getting younger and he's getting older. We're swapping.'

'Come off it,' said Carmichael. 'The age of miracles is past. I'm just jet-lagged and you're looking pretty good, but it's probably just not having to live with Dad any more.'

*   *   *

A man came out of the bedroom, dressed in good shades of black, but as if he were living four or five decades back, not now. Carmichael put him as in his early forties.

'Well, Mum,' he said, '. . . is this the one you wrote to me about or is it a new one?'

'Carmichael!' said Grace, shocked. 'Of course it's the same one. What do you think I am? This is Walter Wells, the painter.'

Carmichael found he was not so upset at the idea of his mother having sex with a man other than his father as he had expected. Whatever their chronological ages the ones in their head were different. Walter was no gigolo, Grace no older woman being taken advantage of. They looked more like Adam and Eve than anything. He needn't have flown over in such haste and alarm. If Toby played up in NZ he would have his mother to blame. There was no not accepting her as his mother when it came to whose fault was whose: it lay fairly and squarely at the maternal door. As his therapist had pointed out, it is a mother's duty to save her children from their father. Grace should have left the homophobic Barley long ago, when Carmichael's sexual orientation became evident. Some things the therapist had got just about right.

Of course some of it had been Carmichael's fault. He should have relayed the contents of the phone messages from the mistresses years back. But once you start hiding things it is hard to stop. And he hadn't wanted to hurt her. He'd assumed that when Barley got to his mid-fifties he'd stop playing about. And Grace had been punished enough.

Though, actually she seemed to be having too good a time: almost as if she had reverted to an age before Carmichael was in existence. The carefree life of the unchilded, who having nothing better to do than have a good time, spend money, and consider their innermost feelings. It was spooky. Elderly divorced mothers are not meant to look like Eve.

They ordered in a pizza – a *pizza?* his mother had never in all her life brought in a *pizza* – and drank red wine. Australian, what was more. Carmichael raised the age issue and asked if Grace had seen a doctor about her fears. It was always possible there was a rational explanation. What with the completing of the human genome, and the kind of interference now possible into the process of ageing, who was to say what went on? What was in the drinking water? At least in Oz you could be sure of unpolluted tap water: one of the reasons he'd gone to Sydney was for the Blue Mountain water: in London it had been filtered through the kidneys of Reading and Slough once or twice by the time it got to the taps of WC1, and was still full of oestrogen from the birth pill girls took between babies, which couldn't be filtered out. It was well known there was a greater concentration of young middle-class, health-conscious mothers in Reading and Slough than anywhere else in the country; God knows what they were all taking these days. Longevity pills, perhaps.
'You're talking too much,' said his mother. 'Just like old times. God, it's good to see you again, Car.'
She never called him Car.

Walter Wells said it was an ingenious solution but he thought it was more complicated than that. He was a bit of a pompous git, thought Carmichael. Though Carmichael wouldn't throw him out of bed if he was that way inclined, which he doubted. Mum had done pretty well for herself. She was right, Walter Wells did look a bit the way Carmichael hoped to look, fifteen years on. Hair not too much receded, an air of competence, of being in charge, attractive to all genders. Walter drank a good deal less than Grace, Carmichael noticed. At least there was someone around to stop Grace hitting the bottle, which had always been on the cards. Sometimes when he was small she'd been quite drunk when she put him to bed, slurring over the words in the children's story she was reading to him. The therapist had made quite a meal of this too.

'I have been to see a doctor,' said Grace. 'But they won't admit the evidence of their own eyes. And they say their equipment is faulty if it comes up with any answer that they don't expect.'

'Perhaps we need to take you to an alternative healer,' said Carmichael. 'Someone whose mind is open, not closed. Preferably a non-European. In Oz you get to realise just how hidebound this old country is.'

35

What a thrill to see Carmichael at the door, and looking so strong, healthy and almost, dare I say it, heterosexual. At any rate he's stopped being closety and chippy and feeling the reason for this, that and the other is his gayness. I daresay Barley would have found some other reason for being dismissive of him. Fathers do. And Carmichael was always so good-looking if he'd only stand up straight and look you in the eye, and now he does. The wide-open spaces have done him good: he has filled out to fill them. So difficult in gloomy, narrow, grimy Soho to stride about being yourself as you can in Sydney's Kings Cross. I don't know if Carmichael is totally happy with this Toby of his: he doesn't seem secure in his affections, not as Walter and I are, but perhaps we set impossible standards.

Carmichael came at an opportune moment. Walter and I had been standing in front of the mirror naked, looking at one another when the knock came, and then another and then the long peal of the bell. I'd just got out of the bed and glimpsed myself in the mirror – which for years I've hated doing – and had stopped to stare in amazement.

There I was, long-backed, slim, high apple-breasts: had I ever looked like this when young or was this someone else's body altogether? And Walter, also naked, stopped and stood beside me. He wasn't just a slip of a youth any more. His hair was receding: he looked intelligent rather than ingenuous. He was turning into a variation of his father, which sooner or later he must in the end do, and which they say is 'natural', but seems pretty peculiar at the best of times. If we are all so temporary, what is the point of so much individual consciousness? As for myself, whatever was happening to me was 'unnatural', that is to say without any precedent that I so far knew about.

We saw one another as the mirror saw us, with more truth than either of us could manage on our own, and turned to each other and embraced. We both knew in our hearts, I think, that the only thing that would stop this reversal was to desist from lovemaking. We also both knew we would neither of us do any such thing. And that not to desist was a kind of slow suicide. For I would get younger and vanish away at one end of the scale, and he would vanish away at the other, and into what great silence.

And then the door-knocker banged and banged and the bell rang and rang.
'Perhaps it's Ethel come back with the tape,' I said at first. But I knew she would never bang or ring so hard. Ethel, though brave, was tentative and a little ingratiating in friendship, not noisy and full of demands. The missing tape betokened a lost friend: she had betrayed me but that was the worst of it. The only person who had anything to fear from the tape itself was Doris, and if she wanted to pay for it, then lucky old Ethel. What was more, Ethel had vanished, which

was not without its good points, since it left the Tavington Court bed free for Walter and me, should we so decide to use it, as we just had. And there was no way my love for Walter was going to be shaken, no matter what was on the tape, no matter what Doris had contrived to make him do in the forgotten hours. We had lost all interest in hearing it.

The outside world demanded entry and I went to open the door, admiring the smooth white fingers of my hand as I did so – had I really had such lovely hands as a girl? Perhaps so, but who had been there to notice them except Barley, and he wasn't given to compliments. All Walter had to do was raise my fingers to his lips and they turned beautiful. Perhaps Walter was creating me as he created Lady Juliet on canvas, and myself, and now Doris, or at least part of her. Perhaps I was the subject of an artist's ploy and not the cause of it. Perhaps Walter created the world around him to fit in with his vision of it, and I now had no real identity outside his love. Without it, I would just fade away, like a pixel on a computer screen when the power's turned off. Perhaps this was all his doing, and none of my responsibility. Barley used to boast that he created me. Now Walter was un-creating me.

But I opened the door to Carmichael and doubt faded. I was Grace Dorothy McNab, girl of this borough, and what is more I was a mother, and this was my son. And all manner of things would be well.

Carmichael took us to a Chinese medicine clinic in Soho for our cure. We were to queue up like anyone else. There was nothing so special about us, and nothing new under the sun. In ten thousand years of treating ailments something like this was bound to have come along, said Carmichael, and the cure to be within the encyclopaedic knowledge and tradition of the healers of China.

36

Barley called by Tavington Court just to see how Grace was getting on. It did not occur to him that she might be out: he knew that she was in a relationship with Walter Wells, Lady Juliet had told him as much, and indeed Sir Ron when he finally lunched with him at the Connaught, as if to say 'now see what you've gone and been and done'. He would have liked to have taken a stroll through central London with Doris but these were fewer on the ground than they had been, and perhaps it was just as well, because they could turn out expensive. Doris was up to her eyes in work.

Flora had been offered her job back but refused to take it, and now Doris was up a gum tree, having to run round and do all the dogsbody work herself. All the artists in London wanted to be on the *Artsworld Extra* show: there was no shortage of willing subjects for the *Night In the Life Of* slot, painters, sculptors, poets, happy enough to live and work – even, as Doris once bitterly observed, shoot up and shit – with cameras trained upon them, and skilful editing could make all of them look okay, it was the studio guests who were the problem.

Doris needed briefing, and now there was no-one reliable to do it. Astonishing the number of researchers who made a hash of the simple task of asking someone what they thought and passing the answers up the line. There Doris would be, on air, expecting the guests to have one opinion and they'd say the exact opposite, and the blazing public row relied upon would simply never happen. Flora had let her down badly. It was no use Barley saying she had to learn to delegate: who was she meant to delegate *to*? So no more pleasant walks through London as if there was all the time in the world. There wasn't.

Perhaps Grace would be up for a stroll. Two years after a divorce, for most people, was surely enough time for any animosity to calm down. Grace had turned out to be less like most people than he supposed. Sometimes he felt he'd been married to a stranger all those years: that she'd deceived him. So of course he'd found himself looking elsewhere, what man wouldn't, what else did a man want wealth, power and status *for*, but to have his choice of available women. But he'd never let it damage the marriage: he'd always pulled out if things began to look serious – until Doris. Doris was not to be taken lightly.

There was nothing at the office which required his immediate attention. That in itself was not a cause for concern. It simply suggested he had delegated well. Opera Noughtie had, it was true, gone rather ominously quiet. Lunch with Sir Ron had been relaxed and easy, but these men were trained beguilers: they'd stab you in the back and keep smiling when the knife went in. He'd brought the subject round to Makarov: yes, that had been him in the car: what a coincidence! Lady Juliet was going to Leningrad, and Makarov was helping with a few arrangements. No, not a holiday, she was going over for the Spick and Span Trust, another of her charities. Spick and Span funded heritage preservation projects – temperature regulation, damp control, that kind of thing – and the Hermitage had just discovered a new batch of art treasures in one of the back rooms on the fourth floor which were badly in need of help. Lady Juliet had actually got a couple of million out of Makarov: 'These men of steel – or shall we say in this case uranium, ha-ha – are suckers for the arts all over the world. Well, you'd know all about that, Barley!' Not exactly a prod in the ribs and a 'you old dog, you' but getting there. Being married to Grace had never excited envy: being married to Doris did. He hoped to God it would not tell against him in the corridors of power. Who'd have thought the old bat was capable of stirring up so much support: the prison sentence had done it, of course, turned her permanently into a victim, and everyone these days loved a victim, hated a victor.

No need to bring the subject round to Billyboy, Sir Ron had done that for him over grilled Dover sole. So much amazing food on the menu, and so little anyone could eat these days, they agreed. They ate up their broccoli manfully.

'Billyboy may be going bust,' said Sir Ron, casually. 'Overstretched himself. Not so much lewisite about as he thought. A couple of the fifth-division nations have already reneged on the treaty. They're simply dumping the stuff down the nearest mineshaft and to hell with the water table. Who wouldn't, if they could get away with it.'
'Including Billyboy,' said Barley. He couldn't help it.
'Yes, have to keep a close eye on him if he sets up shop over here,' agreed Sir Ron, affably. 'A real charmer, though. Juliet's had him round to dinner a number of times. You and Doris

have to come round one evening. Though I imagine she's kept busy at her work. TV wreaks havoc with the social life.'

'I heard Billyboy was thinking of going into partnership with Makarov,' said Barley, pressing home his advantage of not having been asked to dinner recently.

'My lewisite, your nuclear waste, ha-ha,' said Sir Ron. 'Makes sense. But think of the row. The Nimby factor. Not In My Back Yard. Too much time wasted in consultation over here. The French do it better. *Si vous voulez drainer* ze lake, do you ask ze frogs? Anyone who lives near a nuclear power plant in France gets free electricity. That soon shuts 'em all up.'

Which was about as much comfort as Barley could get. Now he was disappointed to find from the porter that Grace was out. He was glad to see she'd chosen somewhere sensible to live: somewhere solid and respectable, as befitted someone in her position. He thought of Wild Oats, now no more than a building site, and almost envied her.

Doris had promised the place would be ready for his birthday. He doubted it. He knew builders better than she did, and how the more you pressed the more like quicksilver they became, scattering in all directions. And he'd never known strong-arm tactics to work. Like weighing in Ross every Friday under pain of the sack just made him eat more. People were like that. Sensible people never confronted a builder, they understood that quotation was not an exact science, that client and builder were in this together, sharing the risk. Look beneath the surface and God knew what you'd find. My house and money, your skill and hard labour. Things were done the way they were done for good reason: custom and practice might appear inefficient, stupid and slow but they took into account vagaries of human nature, weather, landscape and dry rot.

As for birthdays, Doris cared about birthdays, he did not. Doris needed presents, money spent, fulsome congratulations on having come into the world, and a whole lot of special attention paid to her. He'd grown out of all that long ago. How old would he be next birthday? Fifty-nine? Intolerable, and best forgotten. Age was bad for business.

'She's out with her young man,' said Mr Zeigler. 'Not to mention the other one who said he was looking for his mother. Miss McNab doesn't look or act like anyone's mother, let me tell you that. In and out of here like yo-yo's, not to mention the girlfriend. Goes out for ten minutes and comes back with a geezer from abroad with a tiepin. She didn't look his type to me, but some men prefer a midi skirt to a mini, when all's said and done.'

Perhaps the change of name had affected her in this way? From Mrs Grace Dorothy Salt, back to Dorothy Grace McNab – Barley had never liked Dorothy so when they'd married she'd taken on Grace at his request – had been too sudden. She was taking up her old self again, being the person she was before she married, and if that person was seventeen, too bad. It was his, Barley's, fault. He had asked Grace to go back to her original name for no better reason than because Doris wanted her to, and Grace had said yes, it being in her nature as it was not in Doris's, to do people a service and not a disservice if she possibly could.

Barley asked Mr Zeigler to tell Grace that her former husband had called, and Mr Zeigler said he was not a message service, muttered something about dirty old men, but agreed to do so.

*   *   *

184

Ross was parked on the other side of the narrow road, against a long stretch of fence, on double yellow lines. The lines, on both sides of the road, ensured that few came down here, except taxis dropping old ladies off, and delivery vans prepared to risk the traffic wardens. Barley emerged from the double doors of Tavington Court, walked down the wide shallow steps, and stood for a moment on the edge of the kerb. A black off-road Jeep came out of nowhere full at him, mounting the kerb at speed. He leapt backwards for his life up the steps; chrome bull-bars skimmed the edge of an Edwardian lamp-post with a screech of impacting metal, and the monster accelerated erratically away. Ross got out of Barley's own car, red faced. Mr Zeigler came out of the doors. Barley stayed flattened against the brickwork for fifteen seconds or so, shocked.

'I saw that,' said Mr Zeigler, accusingly. 'Someone's got it in for you. You're mixing with the wrong people.'

He went back inside. Ross held the rear door open for Barley, short of breath and panting, but his colour was returning to normal. Barley got in the back. Ross switched on the engine and drove off.

'That wasn't an accident, was it,' said Barley, presently, from the back.

'What else can it have been, sir,' said Ross, surprised. 'Nasty, but these things happen. Foot on the accelerator not the brake, most likely. Some automatics will do this surge thing when you start them from cold.'

'Uh-huh,' said Barley. People drove those things because they didn't have automatic gears, and it certainly hadn't been starting from cold. Perhaps Doris was right. He needed a younger, fitter man than Ross at his side. You couldn't just fire people these days. You had to show good reason. Ross had flunked out.

'I always thought,' said Ross, 'it might have been something like that with Mrs Grace when she went for Mrs Doris. Easy enough thing to happen. But people will have their pound of flesh.'

Barley wasn't listening. Accident or otherwise, the happening was bad news. Either God wasn't on his side, putting him in the way of singular bad luck, or the Russians knew something he didn't, and were expressing their displeasure. One way or another, he would almost rather it was the latter.

37

The window of the Chinese medicine clinic in Dean Street was dusty, decorated with scarlet paper tigers and cardboard lotus flowers. Tubs of herbs had remained undisturbed for many years, and a notice in French warned against snakebites but proposed a remedy. Many flies had flown into the space and not flown out again. But Carmichael said they'd cured him of his asthma after conventional methods had failed. I had not known that Carmichael had ever suffered from asthma but he assured me he had. I had simply failed to notice. But that was all in the past: he could see now how unhappy I had been with his father and how hard it had been for me to focus on the needs of a growing child. He had his mobile phone with him and kept trying to raise Toby in New Zealand, then calling the telephone company to find out why the call didn't go through, though Walter pointed out that a mountain in New Zealand might well not have a signal. Carmichael claimed this was blatant anti-antipodeanism on Walter's part.

Further inside all was neat, clean, sparse and hygienic. Calendars showed laughing children in the New China. Grave-looking young men in white coats weighed and measured out dried herbs, barks and seeds from dispensing units. A supervisor checked their activities. Patients of all races, looking no better and no worse than those who attended my local conventional surgery, received their brown paper bags and went hopefully away.

Walter showed his uneasiness. Like so many men he was not good at letting others know better than he did, medical training or not, and felt his willpower alone should be enough to subdue his body.

'This is a bad idea,' he said. 'Not that I'm not grateful for you showing an interest, Carmichael. But now I come to think of it I had a great-uncle that suffered from premature ageing. It's probably a mild dose of something like that, and I've inherited it. Fluctuation in age is hardly a catching complaint, like the measles. Shall we just give up and forget about it and go home?'

But Carmichael said there were more things in heaven and earth. And then it was time for us to go in, and for Carmichael to go off to the pub to meet his friends and no doubt encourage them to emigrate to Oz. He was like his father in his charm and enthusiasms, and I found myself very pleased with him, and bounced into the consulting room, Walter following stoically behind.

The clinician listened seriously to what I had to say, and put up with Walter's caveats and interjections, nodding and clucking as if he had heard the tale, if not often at least once before. Carmichael was right: there is nothing new under the sun. He felt our pulses and the glands in our necks: he stared into our eyes, asked questions about our diets, made notes and wrote out a different prescription for each of us. We went away with our brown paper bags of mixed organic substances, which smelt strongly of liquorice. We were to boil up the contents three times on three consecutive days and each time reduce the mixture to a third of its original volume. It did not matter what that volume was to begin with. Then we were each to take a tablespoonful three times a day for three days and we would be cured.

As we left, the clinician came out of his surgery and said, 'Ha! Good to see brother and sister together.' Which made me think perhaps he had not quite understood our predicament, but Walter had not heard and I did not mention it.

'More like magic than science,' he said mistrustfully on the way home, and I shivered. I do not like messing with magic. Perhaps someone had put a curse on us? Who? There was a young girl from Haiti in prison with me, who accused me of staring at her, and poked two fingers at me as if I were the devil and wished misery on me. I had been staring, it is true, if only because she looked so desperate and beautiful, a great knot of glossy black tumbling hair on top of her head with a red ribbon in it, which nobody dared take away in case she bit them, a slender, glossy body and a lovely face. But I didn't think it was her. She was insane and howled a lot and practised voodoo in her cell. I didn't think the curses of the insane could make much impact. It could be Doris but she had more obvious ways of expressing her obsession with me, such as trying to seduce Walter. And it would be her instinct to age me, rather than the opposite.

When we got back to the studio, Ethel and a man whom she introduced as Hashim were sitting on the stairs. I was so pleased to see her, to know that she hadn't been planning to blackmail me – on the contrary, it seemed to have been their impulsive plan to blackmail Doris. I could have told her this

189

was not likely to work, but they had found out the hard way. Hashim, whom she seemed to have picked up in the street outside Heals, and taken back to Tavington Court in order to earn some money, turned out to be a security guard at the TV company where Doris worked, and no friend of hers. She was popular with the public, it seemed, but not with colleagues.

Walter was rather shocked to find that Ethel 'walked the streets' as he put it, in a rather Victorian way, but I had to explain that in prison one just learns to be practical. After they've strip-searched you a couple of times what happens to what part of your body ceases to be disconcerting. Having babies has much the same effect: everything in public view, teams of doctors and nurses, male, female and in-between. What's the odds thereafter. I was sure Ethel wasn't going to make a practice of it. She'd had beginners' luck, as it happened, and found Hashim, who seemed to want to stick, so now she preferred to offer her services for nothing. And in a way it had been my fault – if fault there was. I had lent Ethel the flat but not bothered to ask if she had enough money to buy food or drink, and there was next to nothing in the fridge.

I didn't ask them what was on the tape. I kind of knew. I also knew that Walter had recovered from whatever vague miasma of longing Doris had cast over him, and which was what had so drawn Barley to her. To be a *femme fatale*, it seems, a woman doesn't have to be in the least mysterious, sultry or sleepily exotic: there just has to be a gap between her and nothingness which is greater than it is in most other women. Such creatures do stalk the world and it is one's misfortune to run into them. They know no morality, or only that of self-interest. She had cost me my marriage but given me Walter. Her portrait was finished now, and stood with its face to the wall. The body had been slimmed down satisfactorily, and the Bulgari necklace still glowed from Lady Juliet's white and perfect bosom. Walter said he was not proud of the work, but neither was he ashamed. He felt at one with Goya. The shifting and loosening of the paint had stilled: Doris kept the face Walter had given her, repaired and steadied with a prophylactic layer of varnish.

Walter had resolved not to tell Doris the portrait was finished until he absolutely had to: she might try to beat him down because the transformation had been too quickly achieved. When people buy a painting they like to feel they are buying a piece of the artist: his genius, his life, his time, his agony. If it's easy they don't want to know. Whistler, asked how long it took to paint his mother, replied, 'a lifetime'. He knew better than to respond in terms of weeks, let alone days. Besides, it was true.

The Manhatt. Gallery had asked Walter to ship over another six canvases, early work if possible, but since most of these canvases had been sold, except a few he could not bring himself to part with, he was now faking his own early style, a process he found fascinating, though from time to time he would mutter 'puerile' as he applied his brush.

We boiled up our Chinese distillations over the course of three days and dutifully swallowed the dark and turgid liquid. It made not the slightest difference to anything. I went on looking lovely in the mirror and Walter looked more and more responsible. It may have not been that the medicine was a failure: it might have been that we got the saucepans mixed at some stage, and Walter drank the stuff that was meant for me, and I for him, and one way or another we neutralised the effect. We did the boiling up and reducing over at Tavington Court, so powerful and aromatic were the fumes, and Mr Zeigler came knocking at the door, asking what witches' cauldron we were brewing up now.

It was hard for either of us to concentrate for long on the peculiar nature of our ageing patterns: or maintain any level of anxiety in relation to them. There was so much good in every day the problem could at best only drift in and out of our minds; and besides, it seemed like bad luck to focus on it too much. If we did nothing it would go away, if it was there in the first place. It was only when someone like Carmichael turned up or Mr Zeigler made some telling remark that we actually did something about it: or half did.

And then my sister Emily turned up, sent on to the studio by Mr Zeigler. Emily, now aged fifty-two, fresh from the Yorkshire moors, smelling of out-of-doors, dogs, husbands and wood fires, horse-faced, long yellow buck teeth, grey-haired, shapeless tweed suit, sensibly shod, with a squirming golden Labrador at her heels. My little sister Emily! The dog ran past me and straight into the studio, sniffing into all corners, inspecting everyone present, puzzled a little by Hashim, who shrank back in alarm at the enquiring cold nose, and finally sniffing out Doris where she stood facing the wall, confined to canvas. He growled and backed off, his hair standing on end, but then quickly turned his attention to the remains of a Hawaiian pizza, still in its box, left over from the night before and on the floor, devouring pineapple chunks and some of the cardboard before realising what it was. Dogs too must live in the real world, and pay attention to matters of the flesh and not the spirit.

'Why Dorothy,' said my little sister Emily, 'what have you been and done? This won't do. Look at you! You are altogether unGraced!'

192

38

'Darling,' said Doris to Barley, 'I'm giving you a surprise party for your birthday on Wednesday. Do you think it would be a nice gesture if I invited Grace? Just to show the world we're friends?'

Barley looked at her cautiously. His birthday was only five days away. They were lying fully dressed on the Giacometti bed at Wild Oats. Ross had driven them down for a tour of inspection. Barley had to agree that the builders had done an amazing job.

'I just took a firm hand with them,' said Doris, 'and then I brought in a team of TV set-designers from work. So now the architects can whistle for their money. TV builders can put up a whole house in a week, did you know that? I don't know why everyone makes such a fuss. It only gets a temporary licence from the building regs. people, of course, three months or so, but who needs more? We have to live more centrally, this place is way too far from the hub, and the suite in Claridges is quite perfect for everything except big parties. I'm hiring a fleet of cars to bring the guests in from London. Everyone who's anyone, and I'm sure some of them would be ever so pleased to see dear old Grace. We don't want bad feeling buzzing around. Not good for karma.'

'I can see what you mean by a surprise party,' Barley observed, and she giggled and nudged him like a naughty little girl.

'And she can bring along that young man of hers, you know, the painter?'

'Walter Wells,' said Barley. 'I don't know that I'd like that.'

'That sounds suspiciously like that old anthropological thing, mate-guarding,' said Doris, suddenly tearful, 'and Grace McNab is no longer your wife. I am. That really hurts me. You should be happy to welcome her boyfriend into your life.'

He was always taken by surprise at how vulnerable she was, beneath the brisk, confident shell. And now also at how upsetting he found the thought of Grace in bed with Walter Wells.

'If it makes you feel more secure, darling, invite away,' said Barley, nobly. 'Invite whoever you want.'

Doris had not told Barley about the attempt to hold her to ransom at the studio, and he had not told her about the attempt to run him down. Some things are just too complicated to take in, let alone explain, and their lives were increasingly busy. It was especially good just to lie upon the bed for fifteen minutes and relax. Barley noticed that there was a patch of damp on the newly decorated and star-studded ceiling – the stars in the shape of the constellations Sagittarius and Scorpio, in honour of the marital bed – but he did not mention this to Doris in case it set off another manic round of refurbishment.

If Opera Noughtie didn't come through he was finished. There would be no money to start again. None. That is to say not even taxi money across town. And how would their love stand up to that?

'I suppose if we have to have Walter Wells we have to ask Grace,' said Barley. 'But she might be a bit surprised by some of the changes here.'

'It is a surprise party,' said Doris.

The hands of the art-installation waterfall clock had moved to six and it was Friday, and time for Ross's weigh-in, and indeed his, and their fifteen minutes' rest was over. If Doris had once agreed not to subject Ross to the humiliation of standing on the scales she had forgotten: indeed she had now decided to extend the ceremony to her husband. Drastic weight-gain required drastic action, and she wanted him looking good for his surprise party. He'd fallen in with it because he was feeling bad about the Bulgari necklace which would not be ready in time for the very special event which was his birthday party, and the lack of which she was being so good about.

39

Mary House was in Windsor, on the flight path out of London. It was to this convent that Emily now took her sister Grace, convinced that there was something fishy about Grace's over literal return to herself-before-marriage. They were to consult their Aunt, the once young and flighty Kathleen McNab, now the nun Mother Cecilia, aged ninety-eight, who could surely distinguish, if anyone could, what was sent by the Devil and what was sent by God.

They stopped at a garden centre, and Grace bought a wicker basket which she filled with flowers and fruit. This she would give to Mother Cecilia. It was over Grace's arm when she entered the old woman's cell.

It was Emily's custom to visit Aunt Cecilia once every six months. More frequent visits were seen as causing altogether too much excitement. As for Grace, she had allowed the exigencies of her own life to erase all but the vaguest remembrance of her aunt's very existence. The nun in the family had not been much talked about during Grace's childhood: Kathleen had had a baby by her own uncle when she was eighteen, and how is that to be explained to children? The baby died and Kathleen forsook the world, the flesh and the devil and became Cecilia, Bride of Christ, and a source of vague embarrassment to the family. But Emily was dutiful, and visited, and had for thirty years, and now took Grace along.

'If you can visit an old nun, why couldn't you visit me in prison?' demanded Grace on the way.

'I daresay it would have been helpful at the time,' said Emily, 'but afterwards it would have spoiled our relationship. No-one wants to be seen at their worst. I am sure everyone is at their worst in prison.'

'There wasn't much of a relationship anyway,' said Grace. 'You wouldn't speak to me for years.'

'Well you wouldn't sell your bloody Rolls-Royces and help us out of trouble after your Barley had got us into it.'

'The re-sale price is so bad,' said Doris, feebly. They bickered as if they were children again. It was quite consoling. But Grace had noticed, or thought she did, as she changed into skirt and blouse to go convent visiting, that her breasts were shrinking into themselves. It was one thing to be seventeen, she thought now in panic, but who wanted to be thirteen again? Or perhaps she was just thinking herself into it. She didn't feel intellectually thirteen: how could she? She had not forgotten the past, though many had advised her to on her divorce, saying 'now you must look forwards not backwards', and decades of experience must always add up to something. But emotionally perhaps she did. It might just have been her sister's company, of course, and a harking back to the days when they had travelled to convent school together daily, in just such a train as the one which now trundled to Windsor.

'It was the gesture we wanted,' said Emily, 'but you wouldn't give it. You were besotted by ghastly Barley.'

'At least when I was with him I could grow old gracefully,' said Grace. A group of builders at Paddington, working on the gantries, had looked down and wolf-whistled at her: she took some comfort from that.

They had left the dog with Walter for the day: he'd had one like it when he was a child, which he remembered with affection. Ethel and Hashim had both gone down to the Job Centre to find jobs, though how she was to explain her absence from the workscene for three years, and he was to explain his sudden departure from the TV company neither was quite sure. Life can get very complicated, both complained; these days there is no avoiding the personal data that follow after you, from exam results to medical records to driving history to credit-rating to criminal penalty: starting afresh in the name of love can be difficult. They refused to take money from Grace. The tiepin was real gold: it would fetch about seventy-five pounds in an emergency.

Mary House Convent, custom built for its purpose in the mid-nineteenth century, was oddly reminiscent of the torpid Tavington Court, for all its vaulted ceilings and wide pale corridors. The smell of boiled cabbage had got into the walls. At least in the mansion block the walls were steeped with the mixed aromas of Marks and Spencer's microwaveable dishes, or had been until lately, when the fumes of boiled mixed Chinese herbs took over.

Twelve very old nuns now inhabited a convent which had once housed a hundred. Only when the last one died would the premises be handed over to the developers. It was a prime building site, with a fine view of Windsor Castle from the empty top floor, for who was there any more to climb the stairs? In the meantime the Order in Rome stood out against any premature leasing out of even part of the premises as school, arts or community centre, as the local planners would have liked. The prayers of the faithful sustained the world, and the old ladies prayed: it was what they did. There was no-one coming up to take their place. These days spiritual girls, the ones in whose nature it was to deny the flesh, turned into anorexics or trained as social workers. They did not go into convents to live the life of prayer. Once the nuns were gone, once such few threads as still bound earth to heaven had finally snapped, the world would go spinning off to hell, and not stay poised just halfway there. Let God, and not the planners, decree when that would be. Or such was the feeling in Rome, though the nuns themselves, in the front line of the struggle between good and evil, seemed more hopeful.

'Last time I was here,' said Emily to Grace, 'she told me there was now more good in the world than bad. The convents had served their purpose. It's just that where there are angels there are devils as well, and the latter make so much noise the former tend to get overlooked. I'm sure she will be able to help you. She's a bit ga-ga but not too bad.'

Sister Cecilia sat up in her white-painted bare cell, in a tidy bed, looking out over a walled garden of extreme dullness and wetness. She peered out at them through faded but still acute eyes. She was frail but tough.
'That's Emily,' she said. 'I recognise Emily. Looks like a horse, always did. But who's the other one?'
She stared for a time at the basket Grace had over her arm: red Christmas apples, better for decoration than for eating, and the pale unnatural daffodils they manage to get into the shops in

early December. Then she looked up to Grace's face, and smiled and said, with joy, 'Why look, it's Saint Dorothy. She's carrying her basket. Little Saint Dorothy herself, come to visit me on my deathbed! Shall we pray?'

Of course I am not Saint Dorothy. I am Grace Salt, who was foolish enough to give up her name. I am a middle-aged first wife with a young lover living in physical if not emotional comfort in London at the turn of the twenty-first century. Saint Dorothy was an early Christian Martyr who fell foul of the authorities and lived and died in the first century AD. The story goes that she was visited by two apostate women, but she managed to reconvert them, so the Emperor Diocletian sentenced her to be beheaded. On her way to execution a lawyer called Theophilus mocked her and asked her to send him flowers and fruit from the heavenly garden. Whereupon Dorothy simply turned into a smiling child carrying a basket, and offered him flowers and fruit from its depths. A miracle! Theophilus became a Christian on the spot and the pair of them were both then executed. Of such ironies are myths and legends made.

Saint Dorothy was a favourite of the religious painters – and what painter in the Middle Ages, what interpreter of God's creation, was allowed not to be religious – if only, I imagine, because a smiling child and a basket of fruit and flowers is such a rewarding subject to paint.

Perhaps I had heard the legend as a child, or seen paintings of Saint Dorothy, or read about her in *Little Lives of All the Saints*, and forgotten all about it. But after we had prayed to our Maker, the three of us kneeling on the green linoleum floor, declaring our sins and praising the Creation, and asking for our petitions to be granted, and giving thanks to Saint Dorothy, it seemed to me that my blouse was once again having to stretch to cover my chest, and not falling loosely over it. Perhaps it was all in my head, perhaps it was not, how am I to know and does it matter? I was looking down from a different angle.

'I thought she was meant to be bed-bound,' said Emily on the way home. 'She was out of that bed like greased lightning once she'd decided you were Saint Dorothy. She was decidedly more ga-ga this visit than last.'

'I expect she just thinks she deserves a rest,' I said. 'I expect one would, at ninety-eight. Life can be so exhausting.'

'Her knees were good, if shrivelled,' said Emily. 'In fact they bent a good deal better than mine.'

'Practice,' I said, and kept my own counsel. 'A lifetime of it.'

'Anyway,' said Emily, 'it was absurd of us to imagine you were growing younger. People just don't do that. You look about thirty to me, which is peculiar enough, but come to think of it mother always looked very young for her age. It's in the genes, lucky old you.'

'Lucky old me,' I said.

'I just get to look like a horse, like father,' she said. 'When Cecilia was young her teeth weren't anything to write home about either. I expect it was because she was so plain she went into a convent.'

'I expect so,' I said.

When we got back Walter was looking very young and perturbed and his hair was thick and flowing again and he said he'd had a phone call from Doris and we were both invited to the Manor House for Barley's sixtieth birthday, and were to bring her painting down with us.

'She's got that wrong,' I said. 'It's Barley's fifty-ninth.' But I wasn't going to tell Doris that. One can be altogether too saintly.

201

40

Wednesday, December 12th, 8 a.m.–10 a.m.

The morning of the party dawned as fine and clear as it could for early December. All over London chauffeurs from the best hire car firms worked out distances and routes for that evening. It was one of the first big parties of the Christmas season. Anyone who mattered was going, if only because rumour had it that Barley Salt had extended himself and was about to go bust. They wanted to be in at the kill; they wanted to know how his new celebrity wife would take it. Many said it served him right, after the way he had behaved to poor Grace. Few had bothered to call her up or ask her round to anything more than a quick lunch in the kitchen, cancelled at the last moment, or a shopping expedition which never quite materialised. But they'd felt for her: they had. It could have been any of them, except they would have got out of the marriage at the first affair. Gone for the money, the alimony, and lived happily ever after: it was just that Grace was so nice she didn't know how to look after herself and she put up with too much. Which frankly made her rather dull. But dull women can be quite a threat, men seem to rather like them. And there were few enough unattached men around to spare for a rainy day, everyone knew, without Grace nabbing one. But they felt themselves to be on her side, and *Artsworld Extra* had made a fool of itself promoting Leadbetter the way it had: Doris was a celebrity but with not quite the right kind of people. There was more to art than faeces, filtered and compacted though they may have been.

There was for example Lady Juliet's portrait by the young Walter Wells, which hung proudly above her fireplace, looking down at some of the best parties, the ones with the caviar by the bucketful, and Mr Makarov making jokes, and the rather strange-looking Billyboy Justice in tow. The new Salt couple hadn't been to many of those events, it had been noticed. They'd been paying more attention to each other than either could really afford. But Mr Wells might just be the face of the cultural future, Lady Juliet's jewels glittered so, and hadn't Grace actually gone and shacked up with him and lost a lot of weight? While Barley was putting it on.

But here was a surprise birthday party – rather naff, especially since it was Christmas; those with December or early-January birthdays should just shut up about them – but which had brought their student days to mind, and Doris was barely thirty and in TV so couldn't really be expected to know better. What's more she had laid on chauffeurs; and they said the refurbished Wild Oats – ridiculous name to change a house to – was a treat to behold, and that's why they had agreed to go.

Up and down the breakfast and bedside tables of social London the chattering went on. Those who can't live in a village create their own within the city, like calling to like, cellphones crying out for attention, recreating the gossip of the market-place.

10.20 a.m.
Grace and Walter rise from their tousled bed. They have slept later than they meant.

'I don't really think I want to go to the Manor House,' says Grace. 'I think Doris wants me there just to gloat. It is morally my house, in spite of what the lawyers said.'

'I think you should come,' says Walter, 'if only to protect me from her, and because I'd like your life to have started the moment you met me. I want to be sure, the whole world wants to be sure, that you're no longer pining for Barley.'

He runs all the way down the stairs and up again to fetch the newspaper. He finds he has rather more energy than usual, and puts it down to his having finished and sent off the extra canvases to the Manhatt., just in time. As his spirits lighten, so does his footfall. He quite looks forward to the unveiling of Doris's portrait this evening and wants Grace by his side. Of course he does.

So Grace agrees to go to her ex-husband's party, given by the new wife, as a civilised person must in these days of frequent divorce, or how could anyone live for rancour.

11.10 a.m.
Grace goes round to Tavington Court to find her valium, all the same, as well as do the ironing and see how Ethel and Hashim are getting on. She has not had to take tranquillisers since meeting up with Walter. She can only hope Doris hasn't taken away too much of the Manor House's character, but

Ross has let slip a remark or two down at the Health Club which leads her to fear the worst.

'My, you're looking tired today,' Mr Zeigler says to Grace when she lets herself in, by which she imagines he means she's looking rather older than she was. But that's okay: whatever it was has found its equilibrium at around thirty for her and forty for Walter, which could hardly be better. She feels quite confident about that: they are the lucky winners of one of life's great and rare prizes. Call it miracle, call it what you want. Just call me Dorothy.

Hashim has got the job with Harry Bountiful, the one Ross hasn't taken. He is to be a private detective. He says he is applying for citizenship through the proper channels. They explained at the Job Centre that he was eligible. Ethel tells Grace she's starting a computer-graphics course. She boldly ticked the ex-offenders box on the application form they gave her, and such is society's current desire to rehabilitate the wrongdoer she's been given priority status and can bypass the waiting list. Thank you, Grace, for everything.

11.50 a.m.

'Your ex-hubby was over looking for you,' says Mr Zeigler as Grace leaves. 'That man can move fast when he has to.' It looked like a murder attempt to him, he says. He supposes he should be grateful he didn't have to scrape up blood and guts from the pavement. He's been to the doctor for nausea because of the cooking smells, was she aware of that? But Grace is barely listening. 'The Russians!' she thinks.

A full five years now since Grace pointed out to Barley that the Russians would assume Opera Noughtie to be some kind of government-sponsored sex show – costing only the same as the Dome, and likely to get a better return on their investment – and be none too pleased when they found out it wasn't. 'Silly old Gracie,' he'd said, and kissed the top of her head, 'leave the worrying to me.' Now she's frightened for Barley, but when she gets back to the studio she doesn't tell Walter this. At eighteen years of age she would have. At thirty-two she knows better. This is the wisdom of experience.

2.00 p.m.
Carmichael's flight leaves for Wellington, New Zealand. Toby has finally answered his mobile and asked Carmichael to come out to meet him. All is well.

Emily and the dog catch a train back to York. It is as well she is amongst animal-lovers, because nerves make him pee up against the poles in the buffet area.

Grace keeps a hair appointment at Harrods and arranges to have her nails done. It's the only place in London where they don't raise their eyebrows at the sight of neglected nails, and Grace has lately been helping Walter stretch canvases for the Manhatt. She means to buy a dress for the evening but when it comes to it can't be bothered. She will wear her lucky crimson crushed velvet, the one the colour of blown roses. The fabric is coming back into fashion and doesn't even need ironing.

Lady Juliet goes to the bank in Knightsbridge and takes the Egyptian necklace out of her safe deposit-box, puts it in her Waitrose bag with the shopping and takes the Underground home to Victoria. If there's one thing she hates it's wasting money on taxis. She'll wear the white dress she was painted in by Walter Wells.

*   *   *

3 p.m.–4 p.m.

Christmas is coming: the holiday spirit is about to take over. In offices and boardrooms everywhere people struggle to get important things done by the end of the following week. After that phones will stay unanswered, crashed computers stay unserviced, e-mail be jammed with singing greeting cards. It will be the second week in January when the schools go back before normality returns.

At the Department of Trade and Industry a consensus is finally reached about the fate of the Opera Noughtie project. That it was under discussion in the first place is meant to be a secret, but Stock Exchange fluctuations demonstrate otherwise. Sir Ronald leaves smiling and goes home to Lady Juliet.

They manage half an hour in bed. She doesn't tell him she took the Underground. He'd have a fit. She doesn't tell him that after discussion with Chandri she's decided to have a face-lift. Not liposuction, it sounds too horrid. She'll wait until Sir Ron's off on some trip somewhere, and then nip into the clinic and have it done. She's looking forward to the Salt party. She wonders what Doris will wear: she hopes Doris didn't mind too much having her dress auctioned at the Little Children, Everywhere do. She, Lady Juliet, had rather twisted her arm. But it was in a good cause. So much was. It was time she forgave Doris for not answering the invitation but just turning up, and put her back on her party list.

4.15 p.m.

In a quiet smoke-free boardroom top TV management is discussing breaches of security and other delicate matters, not a few of them to do with Doris Dubois. The existence of a certain tape has come to their notice. It came through the post anonymously to the head of Drama and Culture. Employees are free to do what they want with their personal lives of course, but not to bring the institution into disrepute, and certainly not to offer TV exposure in exchange for personal favours. What if the tape gets sent to the newspapers? The uproar could even affect the level of the licence fee. When it comes to the celebrities of their own creation the Corporation must be doubly careful, it goes without saying. But Doris Dubois is a public figure: if they offend her they offend the very public it is their remit to please. There's an in-built contradiction here, as Head of Documentary and Current Affairs points out. There's no such thing as a 'safe celebrity': safe people are dull people, and that's the last thing the public wants. There is always going to be a risk of scandal. '*Children, hold on tight to nurse*' he quotes, '*for fear of finding something worse.*' Everyone turns to look at him and he realises that to support Doris is from now on to be suspected of having had a relationship with her. He shuts up. He has not had a relationship with Doris, and nor have most men and women present. But reputation is reputation, and once a girl has one it's difficult to shake off. That's been known since Jane Austen's time.

The discussion moves on. The security guard who ran amok and ended up in Studio 5 – a situation which Doris handled well, and which counts in her favour: they are scrupulous, these managers – turns out to have been an illegal immigrant, and his papers blatantly falsified. The Human Resource Department must be hauled over the coals about this but warns in advance that staffing levels must be increased if they're to reach their efficiency targets. One way and another finding the money for actual programmes begins to be a problem. Here they find their solution to the Doris problem. *Artsworld Extra* is to be pulled as too expensive per head of viewer, as it will most certainly prove to be if the quality-weighting is removed before costing. That is to say, if that old reckoning – sitting uncomfortably anyway in today's non-élitist cultural climate – that a viewer with A-levels is worth 1.2 of a viewer without, is removed from the books. This they will do forthwith. Doris's Head of Department, who has to break the news to Doris, leaves the meeting and is not smiling. He tries to contact Doris on her mobile but can't raise her.

4.35 p.m.
Doris is in South Molton Street, picking up a copy of the flame-coloured dress Lady Juliet wrested from her back at the charity auction a couple of months back. Doris has had the dress especially made up and has already had two dressmakers fired for ugly seams. The one the previous week was a rather beautiful girl from Haiti who gnashed her teeth while she worked and disconcerted the customers.
'I'm sure she's very exotic,' Doris said. 'But she just can't sew. You'll lose more customers than you gain.'
The girl had overheard and pointed two fingers at Doris and been fired on the spot.
Doris feels quite shivery for a moment, hoping she hasn't had a curse put on her. She will wear the Bulgari necklace with the antique coins inset, which should be enough to ward off all evil. She laughs at herself for being so superstitious.

It's a pity she won't be wearing the Egyptian necklace tonight as she had planned, or even its equivalent in terms of cost and jewels which she has on order, but the portrait will show how much better such a necklace looks on her, Doris Dubois, than on Lady Juliet. She looks forward to seeing Lady Juliet's face when the painting is unveiled. Snotty old cow. She wishes she had the kind of parents you could ask along to your husband's surprise birthday party but she hasn't and that's that. If it was just her father it would be okay but he won't go places on his own, and gets angry if asked.

4.55 p.m.
Ross picks up Barley and Doris from Claridges. They have their party clothes in the back of the Rolls. Barley is rather silent. They run into heavier traffic than they had anticipated. Ross takes a back way and they find themselves in an Asian street market hemmed in by angry traders. Ross has tried to force his way through a street where traffic is banned, to the alarm of women and children. Doris gets out to explain that she is Doris Dubois and allowed special privileges in this world but down here no-one has heard of her or recognises her. They stare at her balefully. She gets back in the car rather quickly and shouts at Ross for being a fool. Ross turns round and addresses Barley.
'She's a whore and a bitch,' he says, 'and she had it off with that painter geezer only the other day and we have it on tape. Why you ever threw Mrs Grace out we will never understand. Now there was a real lady.'

Ross gets out of the car and walks off and is lost in the crowd. Barley clambers over into the front seat, takes the wheel and slowly drives forward. The crowds melt, but someone scratches a long scar into the side of the Rolls. He drives fast through a pink dusk, faster than Ross ever did, speed cameras flashing them on their way, and they get to Wild Oats only twenty minutes later than scheduled.

*   *   *

210

5.50 p.m.

'Good riddance,' says Doris. 'You're a brilliant driver, Barley. Take no notice of anything that horrid fat man said. It's the kind of lies and calumny people in my position get. He's a disgruntled sacked employee and at the best of times looked like the kind of man who downloads child porn onto his computer.'

Barley says he has other things on his mind. He is waiting for a phone call on his mobile, which doesn't come. The last thing he wants is to walk into a room full of people wearing dinner jackets and have to fake surprise. But he supposes he has to go through with it. He wonders if it is a good sign or a bad sign that Sir Ron hasn't rung. He looks at Doris and is unenchanted. It doesn't seem to matter in the least who she has or hasn't had sex with, and when.

'You're being very peculiar,' she says but has no time to elaborate. She has to run round checking the caterers and the wine and Barley isn't to come into the drawing room until his surprise birthday gift is on the plinth and she's still waiting for it to turn up. She's shrieking obscenities into the cellphone about where is it after all that.

5.50 p.m.

Walter and Grace are driving to Wild Oats as fast as his banger of a van will allow. He is in no danger of speed cameras. Smoke billows out of the exhaust. The painting of Doris is in the back. The dog must have peed against the canvas or something, because when they turned it around the face was fine, but on the body below the waist paint had started to run again and blurred into the blue background, so that she looked positively fat. Walter had to do an emergency repair before they could leave, using white spirit to thin the paint

211

because he'd run out of turps, and finishing it off with Grace's electric hairdryer. They should have checked the day before: and indeed they had after a fashion but only to make sure the face was okay, since that was where the initial problem had been.

Grace was rather relieved by the panic: it gave her no time to be nervous. Walter kept telling her how beautiful she looked, but her dress, when it came to it, was well on the down-home side and everyone else would be dressed to the nines, especially Doris. Grace did not for one minute believe Doris's promises of sweetness and light all round, but she would face up to the challenge and go. Walter wanted her to and she needed to warn Barley about the Russians.

6.05 p.m.

Barley goes to have a bath, but there is no hot water. He tries all the bathrooms. It seems Doris's TV builders haven't the budget, let alone the time to establish this order of luxury. Cold water comes out at a trickle. Barley goes across the lawn to the guest annexe, untouched since Carmichael used to do his embroidery over there. He was too hard on Carmichael. The world has vastly changed in the ten years since the boy left home: there is altogether less premium put on masculinity, on the manly qualities. Barley can see the absurdity of his anxiety about how the boy was turning out. Carmichael was just one of the first.

Carmichael had called Barley from the airport to say he was sorry he hadn't had time to see him while he was over from Oz, but Hi! next time perhaps. If he could raise the fare Barley might go over to Sydney to visit him. Why should the son have to make all the effort? Why shouldn't the father make some of the running? In Barley's mind the Opera Noughtie project is already lost.

There is hot water in the guest annexe bathroom, but no electricity. Barley bathes in the light from the lamp on the back porch, filtered through slatted blinds. He sees a moving shadow outside the window: it is in the form of a man loading a rifle out of sight of the main house. Barley thinks it is a hallucination, a trick of the light, but when the man can be seen to click the barrel to, and Barley hears the click he realises it is all too true. It is the Russians! He is to be assassinated, probably at the height of the party for maximum effect. He leaps from the bath with a great roar, and bounds naked through the kitchen and into the porch. He does not know what he will do when he gets there but, death no longer seems any great threat, and attack is the best form of defence. The man lets out a howl, drops the gun and vanishes into the dark. Local talent, thinks Barley, that was no trained professional. He shouts for help, a security guard comes running. Barley takes his mobile and calls the police. Doris turns up to see what all the fuss is about and, seeing Barley naked says, 'For God's sake, Barley, you really have to go on a proper diet. I mean a real one not just a pretend one.' And she leaves him to get dressed, begging him to do it quickly before too many people see. She's busy and agitated enough as it is. The white wine isn't cold enough.

7.40 p.m.
The police come and take the gun and make notes and go away.

8.00 p.m.
The first guests arrive and a film crew from *Artsworld Extra*.

The portrait has arrived, Doris has taken a quick look at it and announced herself pleased, and embraces Walter closely, body to body, saying for Grace's benefit, 'God, you understand me. We must do all that other stuff again, one night when we both have more time.' Walter looks uneasy and pleads for understanding at Grace over Doris's flame-coloured shoulder.

Grace manages an answering insouciant shrug. Only the thought of the *Artsworld Extra* team at the Manhatt. Gallery prevents her from launching herself at Doris, hitting, spitting, scratching. If she was in a car she would run her down again, worth prison, worth everything.

As it is she helps Doris and Walter put the canvas on its easel on the plinth and cover it with a kind of veil arrangement, which when a cord is tugged will fall aside to reveal the portrait. Doris has asked Lady Juliet to do the honours and Lady Juliet has said of course. Lady Juliet, like Grace, can always be relied upon to offer a service not a disservice if she possibly can, and besides, she is determined to forgive Doris.
'How do you like the refurbishment, Grace?' asks Doris. 'Barley adores it.'
'I think it's fine,' says Grace. It looks perfectly horrible, but then as she remembers now it always had. You could fill it up with chintz and Persian rugs all you liked, as she had, or lower ceilings and go for Installation Art and Contemporary Gothic, as Doris had, but it would always defeat you. Old houses were like hermit crabs: they were a shell under which a sequence of families lived, all doing their best not to think about whoever lived there before and the fate that awaited everyone. The Manor House was just a hard and particularly obdurate shell. Doris could call it what she liked. She was welcome to the place. She was welcome to Barley too, come

to that. If the Russians are after him Grace had better take Lady Juliet's advice to heart and put No. 32 Tavington Court on the market before the official receivers try to make it their own. She might give some of the proceeds to Barley to help him out, but she might not. He should have let her sell the Rolls-Royces last time it happened. Carmichael could do with a house for himself and his Toby.

'Just fine,' she repeats.

9.00 p.m.

Barley makes his entrance into a crowded room, and acts surprised. Everyone knows it's an act, but clusters round warmly, wishing him a happy sixtieth birthday party. Try as he may to persuade everyone he's only fifty-nine no-one wants to know. On top of everything else he has now lost a year of his life. Grace is there looking fantastic in a reddish dress that looks familiar. She comes forward to embrace him and everyone looks on and smiles, including Doris, and a few think Doris is a good and understanding woman, well-versed in the manners of contemporary life, but most don't. Most do have to agree Doris is looking pretty fantastic, what with the figure, the health, the youth, the confidence, the dress and the necklace with the antique coins embedded in it, as if wherever she moved she made history, which in a way she does.

Grace murmurs in Barley's ear, and her soft breath is sweet and familiar, that he should be careful of the Russians and he says yes, he will be. There is no time or space to tell her more because the *Artsworld Extra* crew is right up there close to them filming, and the crowd is now pressing in on them. Flora is here somewhere, asked because Doris is still hoping to win her back on the programme, but Barley can't see her though he looks.

*   *   *

215

Barley makes a speech saying how wonderful it is to have all his good friends about him at this juncture of his life, and how money and success are nothing compared with family and friends, and how happy he is that the mother of his son Carmichael can be with him at this time of celebration. And so on. Sir Ron is somewhere here amongst the guests, he has heard, but must be avoiding him. So much is obvious. Billyboy Justice and Makarov have won. Barley is finished.

Doris makes a speech about how wonderful and sexy Barley is, and how once she had a drink and drugs problem but how now with Barley by her side she has overcome it. She is so proud to be Mrs Doris Salt. She thanks her parents in their absence for everything they have done for her to bring her to this point in life: they would have been here to help celebrate this wonderful evening, her husband's sixtieth birthday, but they're on a cruise. And now will Lady Juliet do the honours because here is his birthday present, from Doris to her Barley, with all her love. A portrait by a great artist, a sudden new blazing beacon in the cultural life of the country actually walking here amongst us tonight, Walter Wells.

Lady Juliet obligingly pulls the rope and the portrait is unveiled. A gasp goes up, because everyone had expected a portrait of Barley but it's not, it's Doris. To present someone with a portrait of yourself for their birthday is surely a bit uncool, and Lady Juliet is saying from the plinth actually it's Barley's fifty-ninth, not his sixtieth at all. Doris should have known this if she loves him as much as she says, and meanwhile the film crew is moving in for a close shot, and getting in people's way, and there is a hard arc light rather near the painting and something very strange is happening. A silence falls, because the paint is blurring round the edges of Doris's body and slipping from her face and she looks cruel and evil, rather as one imagines the portrait of Dorian Gray to have been. Someone even calls our Doris 'Dorian Gray', and Doris runs towards the camera crew calling cut, cut. Then she runs out into the garden sobbing. And Grace takes it upon herself to shoo everyone out of the room to give Doris time to compose herself. Barley, Sir Ron, Lady Juliet and Walter remain behind.

'That is very strange, Walter,' says Lady Juliet, 'because that's my best Bulgari necklace you've painted on Doris's breast, the Egyptian piece, and frankly after this evening I don't like the company it's keeping.'

9.45 p.m.

Doris, shivering in the garden, thinking nothing worse can befall, has answered her cellphone and been told by her Head of Department that *Artsworld Extra* has been pulled. Doris knows the only reason for this late-night call must be that the Corporation are disassociating themselves from her and fast, that they expect some scandal to break. In her present mood she is not sure that she can weather more trouble. She weeps a little and wonders why Barley is not by her side. She goes inside for warmth and sits on the stairs high up in the house where no-one is likely to come.

10.30 p.m.

In the drawing room Walter has finished explaining himself. The *Artsworld Extra* crew has already been informed and are packing up their portable steel boxes. Their jobs are. not at risk: and at least they won't have to work for Doris anymore. The guests arc having a fine old time talking about the Doris/Dorian fiasco and wondering where this leaves Walter Wells and drinking the remains of the Salt cellars

– ha-ha – the while. There hasn't been as good a party as this for yonks. News flies around, like Virgil's many-tongued rumour, that Opera Noughtie has been axed to give way to the biggest environmentally-friendly de-commissioning plant in Europe: all the pleasures of *schadenfreude* are here. Outside the chauffeurs prepare for a long wait, and turn on their mini TV sets for the late night film, but as luck will have it it's been cancelled and in its place is a repeat of the *Artsworld Extra* Leadbetter show. Some poor programmer will get it in the neck tomorrow for using his own judgement.

10.46 p.m.

Barley asks Grace if she will remarry him if he divorces Doris and Grace just looks incredulous and says she's in love with Walter, hasn't he heard. Barley says that isn't such a good idea because after tonight Walter's name will be mud. Lady Juliet overhears and says on the contrary, this is the way Walter's going to get his name known, the world being what it is, and personally she thinks the whole thing's very funny. She says it's probably the new varnish Walter has been using.

10.48 p.m.

Sir Ron turns to Barley, and says Barley must be feeling very relieved. What about? asks Barley, and Sir Ron says didn't you get a phone call? I asked my people to be in touch with your people, put you out of any anxiety. Rumours had been flying, he knew. Partly his fault for having talked too openly to Billyboy Justice in the belief that he'd keep his mouth shut. Not that Billyboy was much good at shutting his mouth in the first place so much of it having been blown away, ha-ha.
'Ha-ha,' said Barley.
'Opera Noughtie goes ahead,' said Sir Ron, 'and the de-commissioning plant as well, but we're giving that to Wales.

Sop a bit of unemployment up, give the new Assembly something to get their teeth into.' Barley is saved.

11.01 p.m.
Barley's cellphone buzzes. It's the police. They've found the
suspect and it's some stalker after Doris Dubois, a loony, a
woman dressed as man, who used to be a cleaner at Wild
Oats. Doris has had a lucky escape. They have her safely
locked up. Barley calls for a large whisky. He's a rich man
again. He can even have Ross back now he doesn't have to
worry about the Russians: he can afford a driver who isn't
all that fast on his feet. Doris will have to get her own car.
Flora turns up with Barley's whisky. Has Barley heard that
Artsworld Extra has been pulled? She, Flora, is to front its
replacement, *From the Other Side*. No, not Art, Art doesn't
get enough viewers, it's the supernatural, her other interest.
Where's poor Doris, she must be in a terrible state, one way
and another. Barley says Doris is never in a terrible state for
more than ten minutes, or however long it takes her to get
her own way, and Flora laughs and says don't be so unkind.
There is something of Grace about her: perhaps that's why
they all got on so well. She is the daughter he didn't have,
except his feelings are not the kind a man has towards his
daughter. He admires Flora's long beautiful neck and thinks
how much better the Bulgari necklace would look on Flora
than on Doris. He will divorce Doris. If you've done it once
you can do it again. Easy-peasy.

11.32 p.m.
Barley's cellphone buzzes again. It's Carmichael from a transit
lounge in Singapore, wishing his father a happy birthday. Sorry
about the incident outside Ma's flat. He'd come straight from
Soho in a friend's car, all upset about Toby, there'd been a bit

of a tussle in the front seat, and somebody's foot had suddenly gone down on the accelerator, you know how it is.

'Well I don't,' said Barley, 'but I'm sorry you were upset.'

'Thanks, Dad,' said Carmichael happily. 'I'm okay now.'

12 p.m. onwards

A drunken search for poor Doris is held throughout the house. Guests join in. Peals of laughter come from the refurbished rooms, as Doris's ideas of what a house should look like are scrutinised and found wanting, and her builders mocked. Mattresses are bounced upon and scorned. Grace, the first wife, finds herself defending Doris, the second. The bath taps that Barley turned on earlier, to no avail, have started to gush water, flooded the bathroom floor and brought down the ceiling of the master bedroom, star constellations and all. Barley just shrugs. What does it matter? Flora would never consent to live in a house like this. It was not beautiful to begin with. Barley will sell it.

Doris is finally tracked down by a party that consists of Barley, Flora, Grace and Walter. She is sitting drumming her heels on the stairs. She has torn off her flame-coloured dress and hurled it in the corner. She is very cross. She is wearing a white slip.

'Good Lord,' says Flora, 'the midnight thudding on the stairs, the wraith in white? I knew I was right. I knew ghosts could come from the future as well as the past. See, I already have my first programme. What price History of Art now?'

'You bitch,' cries Doris, 'You bitch. You want to take everything I have. But I'll be back, just wait and see, and then you'll pay for it!' But her voice sounds hollow to all their ears, almost ghostly, and the house rejoices.